THE ROCK BOYZ II

Money, Power, & Respect

TWYLA T. PATRICE BALARK
DANI LITTLEPAGE J. DOMINIQUE

The Roc Boyz 2: Money. Power. Resepct.

Published in the United States of America.

Published by Cole Hart Signature, LLC.

Created with Vellum

This series is dedicated to our wonderful supporters! If it wasn't for you all, we would be reading our own work. Thanks for supporting us!!

❧ 1 ❧

D'Mari was in a daze as he walked through the doors. Victoria was crying, along with Alyssa, Anastasia, Hannah, and some other close friends and family. They all tried to comfort one another, but it seemed to be no use. The pain that he felt inside was indescribable. If he could do anything at that moment, he would gladly switch positions with his wife and Aunt Shirley in a heartbeat. Mari's knees got weak and he almost fell, but something or someone stopped him. His brother whispered in his ear and told him that he had him. It was packed, but Mari didn't recognize any of the people. D'Mari looked at the people around him and reality set in when he saw J.R.

The week before had been a nightmare. On top of the shooting, Lexi cried so hard and had panic attack after panic attack that she forced herself into premature labor. Once they had her in the delivery room, total chaos erupted. Lexi started hemorrhaging and they were unable to stop the bleeding, causing both Lexi and the baby to lose their lives. The entire family had been hit all at once. As wrong as it may have been to think, but once their loved ones were laid to rest, the entire city of Atlanta was about to feel the wrath of the Rock Boyz and neither of them gave a fuck who lived or died. Even through his pain, D'Mari had to think logically. He knew that they all were hurting, which was why he made all of the guys stand down. Victoria was strong, but deep down, Mari knew that she blamed them for what happened to her family.

The walk to the front of the church seemed so long. With each step that he took, his heart ached a little more. A pastor was reading a scripture, but Mari couldn't process shit. When he reached the front of the church and saw three caskets, he froze. The usher motioned for him to continue forward, but his feet wouldn't budge. Instead of going all the way to the front, D'Mari went to his left and sat on the front pew. For the first time, tears fell from Mari's eyes and there was nothing that he could do to stop them. He didn't have the strength. He just stared at Drea's lifeless body and tried to wake himself up from the dream, but he couldn't.

"TO THE HOLIDAY AND MITCHELL FAMILY, WE KNOW THAT there are no words to comfort you, but you all are in our prayers and we know that God is the comforter. May he give you all peace during this difficult time. We will follow the program as printed," the preacher said.

A scripture and prayer was read, and then the preacher announced that morticians would be closing the caskets momentarily and asked if there was anyone who wanted to have one final viewing. Mari knew that he needed to get up and get some closure, so he rose to his feet before he talked himself out of it. The casket closest to him was Aunt Shirley's. Mari thought about how crazy she was, but she was always the life of the party. In the middle was Lexi and her baby girl, whom J.R. went ahead and named Shirley Junior because of the circumstances. Tears flowed freely down

Mari's cheeks as he made his way to the final casket that his wife was laying in. He stopped when he heard Ava crying and looked back. Mari motioned for Hannah to bring her to him and he also signaled for Victoria to bring DJ. He was aware that they had no idea what was going on, but it was only right that they saw their mommy one last time. Mari held the twins in each arm and a lump formed in his throat.

"I'm so sorry baby... I'm so sorry!" Mari cried and felt himself going down.

"MARI... MARI... D'MARI MITCHELL WAKE YO ASS UP!!"

"Wha... what. What the fuck?" Mari sat up and looked around.

"Nigga whatever the fuck they doped you up wit got you going crazy," Mani told him.

Mari looked around the hospital room and remembered how he acted a fool when they arrived at the hospital. His brother was right. Whatever they gave him made him crazy because that was the worst nightmare ever. D'Mari snatched the IV out of his arm and made his way to check on his wife.

2

J.R. stood in the middle of his residential street and fired shots as the car sped away. He hadn't even had time to wrap his mind around the fact that his baby sister's finger was just delivered to his front door. Once the shots stopped, the sirens began and the screams from the people he loved grew louder. J.R. paused briefly and looked on the porch as everyone panicked. He jogged back towards the porch when he noticed Drea and Aunt Shirley laying on the ground in blood. His heart dropped when he looked over at Lexi, who had made her way over to Aunt Shirley; she was losing her mind.

"GET THEM IN THE FUCK'N' CAR NOW!" J.R. yelled but nobody moved.

"GET THEM IN THE MOTHERFUCK'N' CAR NOWWWWWW!" He screamed again, this time making everyone move their feet.

D'MARI PICKED UP DREA AND RUSHED HER TO HIS CAR. J.R. walked over to Lexi who was hoovered over Aunt Shirley and pushed her out the way. J.R. picked up the woman who he had grown to love and ran her to his truck. Thankful that his back doors was open, he gently laid her on the backseat while Lexi got in the back from the other side.

The police sirens grew closer but his porch and yard were cleared, and everyone was headed to the hospital before the first cops arrived on the scene.

"GOD PLEASE DON'T TAKE MY SISTER AND AUNT SHIRLEY. Please God please." Lexi cried from the back as J.R. drove the shoulder on the expressway all the way to the hospital.

IT KILLED HIM SEEING HIS GIRL LIKE THIS AND HE BLAMED himself fully for all the shit that was taking place. J.R. was not the religious type, but he couldn't stop himself from saying a quick silent prayer to the big homie above.

Both cars arrived at the emergency room entrance about ten minutes later and they reacted quickly. Lexi wobbled into the doors and cried out for assistance as J.R. prepped to get Aunt Shirley out of the car. As soon as he had her in his arms, two doctors appeared and laid her on a nearby stretcher. Looking over, he noticed two other hospital workers doing the same thing for Drea. Neither of them was moving and J.R. knew that it wasn't looking too good for neither his Aunt or sister-in-law.

Leaving his car double parked, he ran into the hospital behind his family. He searched around until he found Lexi and Alyssa crying off in the corner. J.R. shook his head and walked over to them.

"Look, I love the both of y'all and everything will be ok. I need y'all to be as strong as possible. I gotta go handle some shit but I'll be back as soon as I can." He promised before kissing them both on the forehead.

"Jeremy nooooooo! Don't go. I need you." He heard Lexi cry out, but it fell on deaf ears.

J.R. stopped at the desk where D'Mani was and whispered into his ear before sprinting out of the hospital for good. Once back at the car, he got in and sped off to get some answers. J.R. drove like a bat out of hell, disobeying all the rules of the road until he reached his destination. Almost pulling onto the curb, he finally stopped the car. He grabbed his pistol, reloaded the clip, and jumped out. J.R. replayed the moment when he opened the box and discovered Yasmine's finger over and over in his head. Tears escaped his eyes and creeped down the side of his face as he opened the basement door of the trap house. When he entered the room, it was dark and quiet. He flicked on the light, which startled Jessica, who was tied to the chair asleep.

"Get the fuck up bitch!" he barked, removing his gun from his waist and smacking her across the face with it.

She jumped and cried out in pain as she tried to

adjust her eyes but the blood that leaked into them didn't help.

"WHERE THE FUCK CAN I FIND TESSA'S CARTEL BITCH?" HE screamed, slapping her across the face again; this time, knocking both front teeth out.

JESSICA CRIED OUT AND BEGGED HIM TO STOP, BUT IT WAS no good. J.R. planned to get answers and there was no way around that.

"I SWEAR TO GOD, YOU GOT FIVE SECONDS TO TELL ME OR I'm killing all your kids." He promised her.

"LISTEN TO ME JEREMY. I CAN GIVE YOU THE ADDRESS TO their homes right now, but I promise, you wouldn't make it pass the front lawn. Tessa's cartel is not to be fucked with." She replied.

"YOU STILL NOT TELLING ME WHAT I WANT TO HEAR." HE stated, cocking his gun and aiming it at her head.

"LISTEN TO ME JEREMY. LISTEN TO ME GOOD. You are headed down a path of destruction if you act off impulse and emotions. Trust me when I tell you this. Now, their cartel is not untouchable, but this is chess, not checkers, so you have to move accordingly."

For some odd reasons, her words were words of reasoning to him. He had no idea whether the bitch was trying to play him or not, but he was no fool; he knew she was speaking facts. Frustrated and ready to kill someone, J.R. placed his gun back at his waist and paced the floor. Jessica looked on; he could tell she was nervous and didn't know whether to trust him or not but she remained silent.

"Did something happen Jeremy?" she hesitantly asked, noticing the drastic change in his behavior.

J.R. started to ignore her but he figured maybe she could be of assistance after all.

"My little sister….."

"OH MY GOD YASMINE?!" she screamed, almost startling J.R.

"How the fuck you know my sister?" he quizzed, slowly retrieving his pistol again.

"Listen, Jeremy, if I told you the whole story behind all of this, you wouldn't believe me… but I'm willing to do whatever it takes to make sure you and Yas are good."

J.R. LOOKED AT HER CLOSELY AND NOTICED SHE HAD started crying, which wigged him out even more.

"THEY---THEY---THEY SENT ME HER FINGER." HE stuttered, looking into her eyes.

FOR THE FIRST TIME EVER, JESSICA HUNG HER HEAD LOW and wept. J.R. had no idea what the connection was, but he was growing tired of playing Inspector Gadget.

"SHE'S GONE JEREMY. TESSA'S CARTEL SENDING YOU THAT finger was only a warning. If they chopped off her finger, then they have already chopped off her head...." she replied in a low sober tone.

"NOOOOOOOOOOO!" J.R. YELLED, AIMING HIS GUN and letting off one shot.

3

D'Mani sat in his car outside of the hospital, smoking a blunt and trying to wrap his mind around the events of the last few hours. The last thing he had expected to happen when he'd woken up that morning was for him to fuck Cheyanne, and he damn sure hadn't thought Anastasia would pop up and catch him. He honestly thought that they were done, but almost immediately upon seeing her, guilt and regret had set in. He'd barely had time to pull his pants up though before she was flying at Cheyanne. He jumped in front of her before she could connect, which only seemed to piss Stasia off more. In Stasia's mind, it may have seemed like he was protecting Chey, and he kind of was, but not like she thought. He just didn't want her to take her frustrations out on Cheyanne when he was the one who'd made the first move. He was the one who had acted on what he was feeling. Cheyanne may have been a willing participant, but she would have never crossed that line unless he led her to it. Hell, she'd instantly regretted what they had done before either of them knew Anastasia was there.

Then to make matters worse, he'd gotten a call right in the middle of trying to calm down a hysterical Anastasia that her sister and aunt had been shot. Anastasia had stopped fighting him long enough to break down and allow him to take her to the hospital, but as soon as she was around her sisters, she gave him the cold shoulder again. He wasn't sure what had possessed him to even take it there with Cheyanne. Maybe it was some payback type shit, and he just wanted to teach Stasia's ass a lesson. At the time, getting a quick nut and knowing that he'd one upped her had seemed like a good idea, but the minute he saw the hurt on her face, he knew it had been a mistake. As a man, he probably could have lived with what he had done as long as his girl didn't know. However, her walking in on it changed everything and suddenly seeing her at the house with that nigga no longer made him feel vindicated in what he'd done.

More and more, it seemed like them making the move out to Atlanta and setting up shop there was a mistake. Shit had been going bad pretty much since they'd gotten there and now they were in a full out war because he knew that he and his brothers couldn't let this shit fly. Somebody's whole family was going to feel their wrath that much he was sure of. His phone vibrating in his hand brought him out of his thoughts, and he released a sigh at the sight of Cheyanne's name. Knowing that she was only calling out of concern, D'Mani decided to answer and let her know what was going on.

"What's up Chey?"

"Hello? Oh, my God! I'm so glad you're okay! I didn't know what to think when you didn't answer." She shrieked as soon as she got on the line. D'Mani instantly felt bad about stressing her out, but there was no way he was going to answer a call from her while Stasia was right there.

"Yeah, I'm cool. I just couldn't answer cause.....uh."

"Oh." she said, simply understanding what he meant

without him having to say it. "Well, how's your brother's wife and her Aunty? Did you guys hear anything yet?"

"Nah, we still waitin' on them to get out of surgery right now, so they haven't told us shit and you know bro goin' through it." D'Mani found himself telling her, even though he felt as if he shouldn't be.

"Aww poor Mari......" the line went quiet and they both got lost in their own thoughts.

"Look, I apologize for taking it there with you today, that shit should've never happened and--" he started but she cut him off.

"No, I should've never brought the drinks out, and I definitely should have controlled myself better." D'Mani could hear the embarrassment in her voice and felt even worse for putting her in that situation.

"Listen, I'm the one that's in a relationship with Stasia, so I owed her loyalty not you. This is definitely my fuck up, ma." he told her, hoping to alleviate some of the guilt that she was feeling.

"D'Mani I can't let you--"

Boom! Boom! Boom!

A loud ass banging at the window cut Cheyanne off. D'Mani looked up to see an angry Anastasia standing at the door.

"Open this muthafuckin' door D'Mani!" she screamed as she continued to pound on the window with a closed fist. He could barely make out what Cheyanne was saying on the other end as he quickly hung up and went to step out of the car. "Who the fuck yo ass snuck down here to talk to huh?" she jumped right in his face as soon as his feet touched the ground.

"I ain't snuck and did shit Stasia! I came down here to get some air and to get away from that tense ass stare down you was givin' me. That was a fuckin' business call!" he lied and leaned back against the car to put some space in between them.

"Oh, so yo ass couldn't come console me? You wanted to come down here and make a phone call this damn late at night?" D'Mani wasn't sure if the tears that were coming down her face were from anger or frustration, but he knew that she was also grieving her sister, so he had to tread lightly.

"Man listen, you know we keep odd hours Stasia! Don't let that shit from earlier have yo ass trippin'." He growled through clenched teeth. "I'm down here tryna set shit up so we can get at these niggas--"

"Let me see yo phone then." she huffed, causing D'Mani to go silent. He should have known that that was going to be her first request, and it left him no way out. On the one hand, if he showed it to her, she would automatically know that he had been talking to his baby mama, and if he didn't show it to her, then she would just assume that he was talking to her. She held her hand out with her brows raised, fully expecting him to hand it over to her; but he'd quickly figured out that he would rather her assume some shit than to actually see.

"I'm not bouta sit here and go through this shit with yo ass right now! Your sister and Aunty is sittin' upstairs in surgery and you down here worried about who I'm callin' when we not even together!"

"Oh so it's my damn fault?! You actin' like I didn't just catch you fuckin' yo baby mama raw in her kitchen! You think I wanna be worried 'bout this shit? No! I want you upstairs trying to comfort me, but you can't cause you too busy on the phone with that bitch!" her chest heaved as she spoke, letting him know that she was angry and probably on the verge of tears.

"I'm not sayin' that Anastasia, and I told you I wasn't on the phone with her. You sittin' here mad like I ain't catch you with a whole ass nigga in my house! Ain't no tellin' what the fuck yo ass was doin' with him cause you sholl wasn't taking my phone calls!" Now D'Mani was mad! It wasn't his fucking fault that her ass had basically pushed him away and right into Cheyanne. He may have felt guilty, but if they were being truthful, this whole thing was her fault.

"Fuck you! If you wanna be real, I hadn't done nothin' with dude ass! That was a very *gay* ass friend of mine! He hadn't been nowhere near my pussy, but if that's all it takes to make you go out and fuck somebody else then fuck it!" She backed away while D'Mani tried to figure out if she was telling the truth. He really hadn't asked any questions before or after the fact.

"Stasia! D'Mani! Come on upstairs!" Alyssa yelled from a spot right near the hospital doors.

Without anymore conversation, they both took off to enter the building again and ended up catching the elevator before the doors slid closed. D'Mani said a silent prayer that both Aunt Shirley and Drea would be fine before they finally stopped on their floor and stepped off ready to face the music.

4

As the midnight hour approached, the wheels in Corey's mind were constantly turning. The shit that he'd seen and heard throughout the day had him on edge and had him ready to fuck someone up on site. Besides seeing Deana and Janice engaged in a heated conversation, the thought of seeing Janice and the chick that came to see Larry in the stairway discussing something about D'Mani had him suspicious like a motherfucker. Every time he saw Janice after that, Corey stared her down. Normally, her eyes were on him but Janice avoided eye contact with him every time she saw him. The vibe he'd gotten from her was an *uneasy* one instead of the conceited and cocky vibe Janice usually gave off. Corey strolled the hallways in search of the woman from the stairway, but she was nowhere to be found. He thought it was kind of strange that the woman didn't go visit Larry while she was there.

Feeling the sudden urge to check on his family, Corey grabbed his phone and called D'Mani. When the call went straight to voicemail, he thought he might've been busy; but when he called his brothers *and* his wife and got their voice-mails as well, panic instantly kicked in. Instead of the pacing the floor like he usually did, Corey decided to stroll the hallways but bumped into Larry in the hall. The look on Larry's face was one of pure anger and the way he was staring at Corey made him get into a fighting stance.

"My beef ain't with you youngin', so you can come out of the stance, but the info I just received might interest you in one way or another," Larry nodded his head towards Corey's room and they stepped inside.

Closing the door, Corey got right down to business.

"So, what's this info that might interest me?" He posted up against the door while Larry stood a few feet away from him.

"I was having a conversation with a reliable source on the outside, and it was explained to me that me and you got the same enemies."

"Yeah? Like who?"

"It's a couple but the one I wanna discuss is Lou."

Hearing Lou's name again made Corey tense up a bit but his body language stayed the same, which was unbothered.

"What about him?" he shrugged.

"The way it was explained to me was that you were the one that brought him and few others to their demise and that a couple niggas did a drive by on you in broad daylight and almost brought ya life to an end."

Corey started to become pissed as he listened to Larry recite the events that happened with him over the past few months and was ready for his ass to get to the point.

"Is there a point to this man?"

"I just learned that the niggas that tried to kill you is Lou's brother and his squad. His brother resides on the other side town in Jonesboro. He took over all of Lou's businesses and his hunt for you is still on. He got his flunkies searching the

Atlanta, the West End, and Adamsville for you. I don't know much about him. So, I'm not sure if he's the type to go after families but you better handle him before he finds out about ya shawty or anyone else you're connected to," Larry warned.

"You got a name?"

"His government is Jermaine but he's known in the streets as Blue. I don't have a description but when I get something, I'll let you know."

Corey looked him up and down before speaking.

"Why are you telling me this?" he folded his arms across his chest.

"What?"

"You heard me?"

"I told you because I thought that was something you needed to know. You a cool dude and I wanted to look out for you, but if this is the thanks I get then fuck it then!"

"My bad man. It's a lot of shit going on right now that I'm trying to wrap my head around, but I appreciate the heads up," Corey changed his demeanor and tone.

"Don't even sweat that shit. Like I said, we got a few of the same enemies. So, we gotta look out for each other," Larry stated.

Corey nodded and moved off the door.

"Aye Larry, shawty that came to see you on Thanksgiving, who is she to you?"

"That's my dumb ass sister I was telling you about. The nigga she fucks with used to work for me until he betrayed me, got into my sister's head, and convinced her that I had a drug addiction when shit began to vanish in the house we were staying in. I know that nigga set me up but like I said, I'll deal with his ass in due time," Larry gave him a handshake before he left out the room.

Standing in the door, Corey watched as Janice stomped

down the hall pissed. When she got to him, she stopped a few feet away from him, staring him up and down.

"Can I help you?"

"I send my condolences to your family. It's a shame you can't be there with them in their time of need," she spoke sarcastically.

"What the fuck are you talking about Janice?" Corey asked confused.

She didn't say a word. She just smirked and walked off. Corey watched her as she walked off until he heard someone trying to get his attention. When he saw it was Deana peeking out of the janitor's closet, Corey walked quickly down the hallway, dipping into the closet. Quietly closing the door, Deana placed her hands over his mouth preventing him from talking.

"I just need you to listen. Okay?"

He nodded his head.

"About an hour ago, I heard Janice on the phone talking to someone about somebody being in the hospital. She didn't say who the people were, but she said something about having your home passes denied. I don't know what that bitch has done or how she's involved, but if you need to get outta here to check on your family, just let me know and I'll find a way to get you outta here. Okay?" she whispered.

Again, Corey nodded his head. Removing her hand from his mouth, he remained quiet while Deana wrote her number on his hand.

"Put my number in your phone and text me so we can communicate better. We might get caught sneaking around like this."

Peeking her head out the door, Deana dashed out the closet with a mop and bucket. Corey waited a few minutes before opening the door and heading back to his room. He snatched his phone up from the bed and called his wife who answered on the second ring.

"Hello?" Alyssa sniffled.

"Baby? What's wrong? Why are you crying? I tried calling y'all early but no one answered," he ranted.

"We were all at the hospital. Drea and Aunt Shirley were....they were shot early this evening. They were in surgery but the doctor's told us that they're gonna be okay," Alyssa cried harder.

"Baby, if they're gonna be okay, then why are you still crying?"

"I can't talk about this right now. I'll see you in the morning. Okay?"

"Okay. Get some rest and please stop crying."

Alyssa ended the call without responding. Hearing that his sister and aunt in-law were shot and laid up in the hospital made Corey go from 0 to 100. Thinking about D'Mari, he knew he had to be going through it. He tried to call his brother again but it went straight to voicemail. Corey figured he was probably still at the hospital with Drea and didn't want to be bother. All of the bullshit that was taking place and what he had found out made Corey's head spin. Shit done got real for him and his brother and the more time he spent in rehab, the more he felt helpless. Niggas were searching for him and niggas done ran down on his family. Corey could no longer sit the fuck on the bench and do nothing. It was time for him to get back in the game and this time, he was not going to foul out.

5

The dream that Mari had the night before felt so real that it still had him shook than a mu'fucka. It was 6:00 that next morning and he had yet to lay eyes on his beautiful wife. She had been in surgery for over six hours and the family was notified that she was out, but no one could see her. D'Mari almost got kicked out of the hospital for flipping over chairs and cussing the staff out, but due to the circumstances, they overlooked his irate actions since his brother was able to calm him down. Afraid to go to sleep, he stared at the clock on the wall and watched the minutes tick by slowly. Aunt Shirley was in a room resting. Victoria and the rest of the family had been visiting with her and walking back and forth, praying to be able to see Drea soon. Aunt Shirley had gotten away with a gunshot wound to the right leg and left arm; thankfully, both of the bullets went straight through, but she had to be given some blood and pain meds and was being kept for observation mostly due to her old age. Mari knew that he was going to give the nanny a nice ass bonus for Christmas because she had come and got the kids from Lexi and J.R.'s crib and even dropped Victoria off at the hospital right after the madness occurred.

"Mitchell family?" a black doctor walked out and called out to them, followed by a white nurse.

The expressions that they wore on their faces couldn't really be read and the shit didn't sit well with D'Mari. For some reason, he had a bad feeling that something was terribly wrong.

"I need you all to follow me," he instructed.

D'Mari took the lead and got up followed by a pregnant Alyssa and Anastasia. They met Lexi and Victoria at the door who were coming back from seeing Aunt Shirley.

"What's going on?" Lexi wondered with puffy red eyes and her protruding belly.

"We just going to see what's up now. Come on sis," Mari wrapped his arms around Lexi.

He knew that J.R. was in the streets trying to get answers about his sister. As soon as he knew that his wife was okay, he was going to be right there by his side. D'Mari saw his brother walking back in and he followed them as well. Everyone was aware that the tension was thick between Stasia and Mani, but Mari was glad that they were acting civilized for the moment. Everyone read the door that said "*Chapel"* and froze after the doctor and nurse walked in. Mari hit the wall and then finally walked inside.

"Where my sister at?" Lexi screamed.

"How's my wife?" D'Mari echoed right behind Lexi.

Mari pulled her close to him to comfort her, but truth be told, he wanted to break down his damn self. The room was filled with sniffles by the women and mean mugs by the men as they waited to be briefed on what the hell was going on.

"I'm Dr. Brown and this is nurse Jerae. I know you all are going crazy and wanting updates. We came as quickly as we could. This situ..."

"Why the fuck we in the chapel?" Lexi cut the doctor off.

"It's standard procedure to bring families to the chapel after someone dies. In this case, our patient was pregnant with twins, but neither one of them survived and that is why we are here," Dr. Brown explained.

"Pregnant? Died?" D'Mari questioned in a voice laced with sorrow and disbelief.

"Yes. She appeared to be nine weeks. She was shot twice in the stomach and once in the leg, so we had to perform emergency surgery to save her since the babies were already gone. I will say that she is very strong. She coded once during surgery, but came right back before we could even resuscitate. When we..."

"Fuuccckkkk!!! Not my babies! Our babies!! Fuuccckkkk!!!" D'Mari cried out, forgetting that he was in a hospital as well as the chapel.

"Nooooo!"

"Damn!"

"Poor Drea!"

"My baby! Her babies! Help Lord Jesus!"

All could be heard before the doctor could finish saying his piece. Once everyone presumably had calmed down some, the doctor continued explaining Drea's situation.

However, D'Mari really didn't hear anything else that the doctor explained. He was stuck on the fact that Drea was *pregnant* and he didn't even know. Just hearing that explained her crazy ass mood swings and everything. She was on birth control, but clearly that shit didn't work. He wondered if she even knew that she was pregnant. Mari scratched that thought out of his head because Drea had a few drinks the week before, and there was no way she would have been drinking knowing that she was pregnant. Either way it went, the shit pissed him off that much more. Not only had his wife been shot, they had suffered a major loss.

"You all can visit her, but only two at a time," D'Mari heard Dr. Brown saying.

Mari was ready to see his wife, but he couldn't lie; he really didn't want to see her laid up in a hospital bed because of him. For the first time, guilt began to really eat him up at the thought of the situation. They knew what they were doing, but never did he think their family would get caught up in their street bullshit, especially so early into their quest. He hated the shit, but one thing about it, he wasn't about to let the shit slide. Mari said a silent prayer that Drea would understand. They family followed the doctor and the nurse to the Intensive Care Unit and he heard the Holiday sisters saying that they were ready to see their sister; the doctor was gonna have to let them all go in because no one was willing to wait.

"I'll tell y'all what... if y'all promise to keep it down, I'll let you all go in together since this will be the first time you all have been able to see her. The visit for now is only fifteen minutes, but starting at nine o'clock, each visit is for thirty minutes," Dr. Brown stated.

Mari had already mapped a plan out in his head about how he was going to get around the time limits, but he decided to remain quiet for the time being. He walked into the room and his heart dropped at the sight of his wife lying in the hospital bed hooked up to different tubes and machines. Lexi was the first to run over to her bedside, and she broke down crying. Drea instantly woke up and Mari noticed her give her sister a weak smile.

"I'm sorry Drea... we shoulda stayed in the house," Lexi cried.

Mari felt bad that she even said that. There was no way that he was going to let any of the girls take the blame for the shit that they had going on. He had to inform the guys about their living arrangements also. Everyone needed to be together since they were vulnerable at the moment. Mari walked over the opposite side of the bed and grabbed Drea's hand. As soon as she locked eyes with him, she snatched her hand away. And if looks could kill, he would be a dead ass.

6

J.R. hadn't been to sleep in days; his mind was all over the place. He just buried his mother and now Yasmine was somewhere bleeding to death, maybe even dead. He could paint the city red looking for answers, but if what Jessica said was right? There was no need to even expect Yasmine to be alive. For the most part, he had been holding it together, well on the outside at least. Truth be told, J.R. was wreck and having thoughts that he had never had before. He had never had something traumatic happen to him, and if it wasn't for Lexi and his baby, he would be with his baby sister and O.G.

The sound of J.R.'s phone ringing caused him to snap out of his trance. He let out a long sigh before declining Lexi's call again. She had been getting on his nerves lately, but deep down, he knew she didn't mean any harm. She was concerned and worried. Everyone around him noticed the change in his behavior, regardless of how hard he tried to hide it.

Since the shooting, they had been staying at a hotel and that shit alone was driving him crazy. Lexi had a gang of shit and was fake ass bougie, so her and her shit had them crammed like sardines. Him and the guys thought it was best that everyone stayed together due to the circumstances, so they were looking at Air BNBs far from Atlanta. But in the meantime, it was another night at Four Season Hotel.

After ending Lexi's call, a few minutes later, a text message rolled in. Shaking his head, he snatched his phone off the peeling leather couch and stared at it. J.R. looked at the preview of the message and shook his head some more. Instead of opening it fully, he slid the bar across and just deleted it all together.

"Aye J.R., we all set down there. She didn't lose much blood. She's extremely malnourished and the dentist is almost done. I don't know what that woman did, but you fucked her up bad. It's shocking she's still alive," Malcolm, the doctor on their payroll, informed him.

"It's all there," J.R. replied, handing Malcolm an envelope full of bills that was twice his salary.

Grateful and scared as fuck, J.R. watched Malcolm haul ass out of the trap house. Before the door could close, the dentist appeared, gave his spill, and J.R. paid him before he fled. After making sure the doors was locked, J.R. headed to the basement to check on Jessica.

"How you feeling?" he asked, taking a seat on the crate next to the bed she laid in.

"Considering the fact that you've shot me in my legs, punch my two front teeth out with your pistol, and damn near put a bullet in my head, I'll say I'm good," her weak voice explained.

"Look, that shot... I had no intentions of popping you. I aimed for the wall on purpose," he replied.

"Whatever J.R.! I'm just grateful," she stated, pausing and staring at the ceiling.

"How is she?" she asked.

"Who is *she?*" he quizzed, raising his thick bushy eyebrows.

"My best friend Kenya," she whispered, lowering her head.

Hearing his mother's name caused chill bumps to form on his dark skin. Jessica had said something previously about his OG but J.R. never got to pry any further. When she said Yasmine's name the day of the shooting, he was so fuck'd up in the head, he didn't question her. Now that he was more level headed, he realized that she was worth more alive than dead; he could entertain her now.

"Yo best friend huh?"

J.R. grabbed the already rolled blunt from behind his ear, took the lighter out of his pocket, and flamed up. The room was silent. It wasn't until J.R. hit the blunt twice before he spoke again.

"How you know so much, yet I know so little?" he challenged.

It was as if Jessica was waiting on him to ask that question because as soon as he did, she started singing.

"Before you were born, Kenya and I were friends. We met when yo grandmother Rose stayed right off Bankhead Highway, in the Center Hill neighborhood. Kenya's old pretty feisty ass had me running these streets and doing all type of shit," she laughed before continuing.

"We met Justin, Grant, and Elliot at Jelly Bean Skating rink the year before you were born. Boy, did Justin sweep Kenya off her feet.... anyways, I started dealing with his brother Grant, and at the time, they were just starting their cartel. They were young niggas straight running shit, that's how they came the biggest distributors on this side today. Justin and your mom hit it off and eventually she got pregnant with you. One day at the drive-in, there was a shoot-out involving your father and you was a baby in the backseat. The shit scared your mother straight, so she made Justin choose. It was either her or the cartel....."

"So the nigga chose the cartel, huh?" J.R. cut her off and asked.

"Not exactly, you see.... He begged Kenya to stay, but she wasn't having it. Your dad was so deep into the shit, he couldn't up and leave so she left. One day.... I remember this day like the back of my hand... one day, she came to my house with you in her arms. She rang my bell. I answered and she just hugged me. She told me that you were the most important thing to her and that she'll fail as a mother if she ever let anything happen to you. Of course, I begged her not to go. I thought of different resolutions for her. I cried with her, but she still left. Kenya and I kept in touch up until you were a toddler, that's when she met Peanut. Peanut swept her off of her feet. A couple years later, she had Yasmine and that's when things changed. Peanut made her choose. He didn't want her to have any type of contact with me because I was a part of the *"old her"* ..... whatever the fuck that meant. Long story short, she chose him, and I haven't spoken with her in years."

J.R. watched the tears flood Jessica's face as she spoke each word. He would usually question some shit like that, but there was nothing about her story that seemed fabricated to him.

"So, Justin, as a man, he just said *fuck his kid*?" he inquired.

"No! He was around financially, he even drove and flew out to see you a few times, but when she got serious with Peanut...... she moved, changed her number..... she just left us all."

Funny how it wasn't until now that J.R. remembered another man being around when he was kid. His mom used to always refer to him as her *"friend,"* but now that he thought about it, it was Justin.

"So, this beef.... Does he know he's trying to kill *me?*" he asked.

"You mean *you*.....as in *his son?*" Jessica questioned with a perplexed look on her face.

"Hell nah, he doesn't know that!" she said, answering her own question.

"The day we met at the shoot-out, I wasn't supposed to be in the car with them. Grant sent them to pick me up, they were like his little henchmen. Grant got a call that someone spotted you in the bar. He called and since they were in the area, they went to do the hit. It wasn't until you bought me here that I began to put two and two together," she explained.

"The streets refer to you and your crew as "*The Roc Boyz.*" Tessa's cartel knows you guys by name and face. No one ever thought that The Rock Boyz' "*J.R.*" was the same as Justin's son "*J.R*", " she continued.

Completely stuck. Her story added up perfectly with the events in his life. His mother cried her eyes out when he told her that he was leaving Philly and moving to Atlanta. She would never say why she hated the idea so much; he just shrugged it off as her just not wanting him so far way. Come to think about it, him and his *alleged* father Peanut didn't look nothing alike nor did they have anything in common. Everything was fucking his head up, but he knew one thing for certain, he's glad he didn't kill that bitch.

❧ 7 ❧

Shit had been crazy for D'Mani and his family. Although they were achieving their goal of making more money both illegal and legit, they still were taking losses, and the bad was starting to outweigh the good. They had been lucky that Drea and Aunt Shirley had gotten away with their lives, but who was to say that they would continue to be? They needed to act and fast before shit got worse and someone actually ended up dead.

In addition to the street drama, D'Mani had so much personal shit going on that he was finding it hard to concentrate on the most important shit. His relationship with Stasia was all but over, and since having sex with Cheyanne, their interactions had become odd and uncomfortable. Neither of them knew what to say to the other whenever he was around her, and it seemed like Imani had picked up on the tension. As a way to avoid that, D'Mani started having his mama pick her up from Cheyanne. He figured it would be easier than having to face her.

"Aye, you good?" a worker named Red asked, tapping D'Mani on his arm. He was currently checking the count at one of their traps, and he'd let thoughts of Anastasia and the situation with Cheyanne distract him from his task.

"What-, yeah I'm cool man," D'Mani lied easily, side-eyeing the kid like his ass wasn't lost as fuck.

"Oh, cause you messin' up yo count." Red gave him a concerned look and then nodded towards the pile of money in front of him. When D'Mani followed his gaze, he noticed that instead of separating the cash into thousand dollar stacks, he had just been placing whatever the counter spit out into neat piles.

"Damn, my bad." D'Mani sighed deeply and a ran a hand down his face. The shit was getting out of hand, especially when it started to effect the money. He started to pick up the piles that he'd fucked up and Red put his hand out to stop him.

"I got it big homie, gone get ya mind right."

D'Mani stopped and looked dude in the eye, unsure of whether or not he should trust him to handle that shit. It wasn't that Red had given him any reason to question his loyalty, but the way his luck was going, he had to side-eye everybody, especially when it came to business; but then again, if dude was on some sneaky shit, Red never would have let him know he was fucking up to begin with. D'Mani finally nodded and gathered his shit to leave.

Once he made it to his truck, Mani ran a hand down his waves and closed his eyes for a second. He was supposed to be getting Imani today, but he didn't want to spend his time with her distracted. Usually, he didn't smoke when he knew he was going to be on daddy duty, but today, his mind was calling for some relief. He rolled up a quick blunt with the stash he kept in his glove box and sparked it up before pulling off. His phone rang and the display in his truck said that it was Cheyanne calling. D'Mani let the call go to voicemail and continued to smoke. It wasn't that he was trying to ignore her or nothing, but he didn't want to make their situation worse by talking to her about anything besides Imani. Seeing that she'd left him a voice message, he made a mental note to listen to it later.

After damn near an hour and another blunt, D'Mani pulled up in front of the house he shared with his mother. He made sure to spray some cologne on and put a piece of gum in his mouth before stepping out and giving a nod to the nigga he had parked across the street. Their mother had initially refused to have security, but after the shit with Drea and Aunt Shirley, he'd insisted. There wasn't no way he was going to leave her open to an attack. So, Bones trailed her while she ran errands and whenever she was home alone; and he had niggas doing the same for Stasia and Cheyanne too. He wasn't trying to take any chances with none of the women in his life. Once he drove off, D'Mani went into the house, where he was met with the sound of that *"Baby Shark"* song playing. He immediately shook his head because she'd worn him out with that song and Imani was about to do the same to her Grandma.

D'Mani walked through the house until he made it to the kitchen where they were putting cookies on a pan to bake. When Imani saw her daddy, she jumped right down from the bar stool she was kneeling on and went over to give him a hug.

"Hey daddy we're making cookies!" she told him excitedly. Despite his previous mood, the happiness on his baby's face instantly had him feeling better. Imani was always so happy to see him.

"Aww, y'all made cookies without me?" he feigned sadness. His mama waved him off and went to stir something on top of the stove while Imani's face matched his and she rubbed his cheek.

"Sorry daddy......but we made some for you."

"Oh well... if you made me some then I guess I'll be alright." He cheesed and tickled her little belly. D'Mani had to admit that he loved the sound of his daughter's laughter. Her smile was everything to him and he was glad that he'd run into them that night at Wal-Mart.

"Stop daddy!" she shrieked and wiggled until he placed her on her feet. "I gotta dress! Wanna see?"

"Yeah let me see it." He watched as she ran off in amazement. As soon as she was out of earshot, his mama cleared her throat to get his attention.

"Why are you still avoiding that lil girl's mama?" she asked with a hand on her hip. D'Mani groaned inwardly. The last thing he felt like doing was talking to her about the shit he had going on with Cheyanne and Stasia.

"I'm not avoiding her, I just don't wanna see her ass right now." He shrugged as he took a seat on the stool across from her, but he regretted it almost immediately when she slapped him upside the head.

"Stop fuckin' cussing, and what you doin' is the *exact* definition of *avoiding* her fool."

"Look ma, some shit-, stuff happened and I ain't really tryna deal with that on top of all the other stuff we got goin' on." Truthfully, Cheyanne was the least of his worries right then. He hadn't meant to complicate things between them, but his biggest concern was getting his girl back and settling his street beef.

"Ohhhhh... so y'all fucked and now you scared to face her?" she gave him a pointed look, and D'Mani couldn't deny his shock. His mama never seized to amaze him with how intuitive she was. "Don't give me that goofy ass look boy... I'm old-er, but I ain't stupid. Anyway, just because y'all done complicated y'all relationship, don't mean you stop communication. She's still your child's mother and y'all need to be able to talk and not through me cause I won't always be here."

D'Mani nodded. His mother had a point. Him and Cheyanne had to get their lines of communication up for the sake of Imani. He was a father now, so he had to think of better ways to handle things than by just avoiding them. "You right ma, but you ain't goin' nowhere no time soon, don't even think like that."

"Tuh! Boy, I ain't talkin' bout dyin'! I'm tryna live my best life! Anything can happen hell, I might meet a man. The hell wrong with you, talkin' bout death?" She rolled her eyes and turned to cut off the food she had on the stove. "I'm bouta go check on yo brother and Drea, I'll be back later. Oh, and talk to Cheyanne today. She wasn't looking too good." She took off the apron she was wearing and started out of the kitchen.

D'Mani didn't think that him not talking to her would have been affecting her like that, but he'd have to give her a call sometime after he put Imani to bed. In the meantime, he pulled his phone out to send a text telling Bones to send one of the guys back to keep an eye on his mama when she left.

"Don't have that nigga following me either D'Mani!" she called out over her shoulder, causing him to chuckle. Her ass stayed twenty steps ahead of him. As she left the kitchen, Imani came running around the corner with a bag from The Children's Place. He ooh'd and ahh'd at the fluffy ass pink dress and shoes with a little heel that she showed him. She was so excited about being able to wear them that he promised to take her on a daddy/daughter date the next day. When his mama finally walked out the door, the oven buzzed, indicating that the cookies were done. D'Mani took them out, so they could cool off before making Imani a bowl of neckbones and green beans with potatoes and corn bread that she'd cooked.

By the time D'Mani had went and finished his shower, Imani had finished eating and was sitting at the kitchen island eating cookies while she played on her tablet. He laughed at her little grown ass and made him a plate while he waited on her to finish her snack. She watched some videos of kids opening up toys and playing with them as she ate which seemed to slow her down, but eventually, they both finished and he was able to get her to take a bath.

Two hours later, Imani was in bed and he lounged around the living room, contemplating on whether or not he should call Anastasia. As much as he'd been ignoring Cheyanne, Stasia had been ignoring him. After that whole shit at the hospital, he'd found out that Stasia had been telling the truth about dude being gay, which made him feel even worse about fucking Cheyanne. He sat there looking at Stasia's number on his screen for another ten minutes before he finally got the courage to press the call button. It rang and rang, and just when D'Mani figured the voicemail was going to pick up, Anastasia's voice came through the speaker, surprising him into silence.

"What do you want D'Mani?" she asked, sounding like she was tired. As if the whole thing had taken a lot out of her. He was still stuck on the fact that she even answered let alone was willing to hear him out. Honestly, he was expecting to once again plead his case to her voicemail box and now that she'd picked up, he was at a loss for words.

"I, umm...shit. I wasn't expecting you to pick up," he told her honestly.

"Look D'Mani, I just spent the last two hours on the phone convincing my friend Anton not to press charges against you, and I still had to cut him a check for the damage you did, even though I should let yo black ass go to jail! I'm not in the mood to play on the phone with you right now!"

"Man, don't treat me like no bitch ass nigga Stasia... you know damn well I'll double whatever you lost."

"Well, when you do bitch nigga shit...." She let her voice trail off and D'Mani tried to control his anger.

"Stasia, I know you mad and all, and you got every right to be, but watch how the fuck you come out yo face at me."

"Or what? You gone beat my ass next? Nigga I wish you would try and lay a hand on me!" she started going off like he'd actually threatened her or something. D'Mani released a deep sigh, beyond frustrated at the turn the conversation had taken. He wasn't trying to fight; he was just trying to apologize and she taken the shit all the way left.

"I didn't say that I was gone do shit to you, maybe I should just call back another time man."

"Maybe you shouldn't!" she snapped and from the silence that followed, D'Mani knew that she had hung up. He didn't know if they would ever be able to come back from the place they were at. After all the shit that she had been through, the last thing D'mani wanted to do was hurt her; but he also didn't know how much more groveling he could do either. That shit just wasn't in him to keep begging no matter how wrong he was. He'd just give her some space while he sorted out all the other shit he had going on, and in the meantime, maybe look for another crib since his mama was talking all crazy and shit.

Since it was too late to try and call Cheyanne so they could have their *"talk,"* D'Mani decided to listen to the voicemail she'd left him. Honestly, his irritation wouldn't allow him to have another uncomfortable conversation anyway. He went into the kitchen and grabbed him a beer as the message played.

"Hey D'Mani, I know things are weird between us right now and that you've been avoiding me, but I have something really important that I need to talk to you about.....if you can please ...call me back."

D'Mani quickly erased the message and guzzled the bottle of beer down. She sounded serious like something was *really* wrong. He just hoped for his sake and hers it wasn't a baby.

❧ 8 ❧

Staring out the window in his room, Corey thoughts were racing a mile a minute like they had been doing all night. The phone call he received from his wife had him on edge. Learning that his sister-in-law and his aunt-in-law were shot had him in his feelings. A part of Corey blamed himself for what happened to his family because he thought his enemy had something to do with the shooting; but being as though no one knew where he was except his family eased his mind, knowing that his enemy had nothing to do with the shooting.

Corey glanced down at the time on his phone and saw that it was fifteen minutes to ten. He wasn't expecting any visits and he didn't have a group meet, so he was prepared to have another boring ass day in rehab. Days like that gave Corey a lot of time to reflect on the shit that led him to be there. Although his sins were forgiven, he still felt fucked up behind the things he had done. The nightmares he used to have about his friend Boosie had finally stopped a few weeks prior. Once Corey began to participate in the meetings, he found himself coming to terms with the mishaps of his past.

With a drug free mind and body, he felt like he was ready to get on with his life and put the rehab shit behind him.

"Good Morning, Corey," his wife's voice caused him to turn around.

"Hey baby," he smiled. "I wasn't expecting to see you today," Corey walked over to her, kissing her cheek.

"I didn't tell you I was coming because I didn't want to give you a chance to come up with a lie," Alyssa huffed.

"What are you talking about Alyssa?" he asked confused.

"I wanna know what the fuck you and your brothers are involved in that got my sister and aunt laid up in the fucking hospital Corey!"

The look of shock quickly appeared on his face, causing his mouth to hit the floor. Standing there in the dumb nigga stance for a few seconds, Corey closed the door, taking a deep breath before responding.

"Alyssa, I know that you're angry about what happened to Drea and auntie and I'm angry too, but believe me when I tell you, you're better off not knowing," he spoke in a low tone.

"Don't give me that shit Corey! My sister and aunt almost lost their lives behind whatever bullshit y'all got going on! Drea lost a set of twins! She lost her babies Corey! What happened to my family is something that is going to affect us for a while! The family is at odds and everything is so fucked up right now! So, unless you want us to start having issues, you better tell my ass something because I'm not trying to hear that *I'm better off not knowing* shit!" Alyssa shouted as the tears rolled down her cheeks.

Hearing that Drea lost her babies behind the shooting caused Corey's heart to break. Nobody had mentioned that she was pregnant, so he assumed that they found out at the hospital.

"I'm so sorry about what happened to your sister and aunt Lyssa. I know you're hurting baby, but believe me when I tell you that you're better off *not* knowing," Corey spoke sincerely.

"So, you're going to fuck up *our* happiness to protect you and ya brothers?"

"If it means protecting you and the rest of the family, fuck yeah. I know that you want answers Alyssa and so do I. You and your sisters are on ten about what happened and I know y'all are ready to fuck shit up and ride out. However, there is nothing that y'all can do about this situation. What's done is done, bae. All y'all can do is to sit back and let us handle this shit, Alyssa and when the time is right, I promise I will tell you everything."

Unable to speak due to her sobbing, Corey wrapped his arms around her as she continued to cry. The pain of his wife entered his body and the harder she cried, the angrier he became. There was no doubt in Corey's mind that the rest of the women were reacting the same way as Alyssa, but he knew that his brothers were on the fucking job searching for answers. That was all the more reason why he needed to get the hell out of rehab.

"I'm scared Corey. I worry about y'all when y'all out handling business. I'm kinda happy that you're in here because you're out of the way, but I need you home. You know I'm gonna have the baby soon, and I don't want to be there by myself, bae," she sniffled.

"You're not gonna be by yourself, Lyssa. I'm gonna be right there with you. I promise," Corey kissed his wife's forehead.

Wiping her tears away, Alyssa pulled herself together. Once she was calm, they sat down on the bed and talked for a few more hours until Alyssa got tired and was ready to leave. As Corey walked his wife to the front, he saw Janice staring at them as they passed. It looked like she wanted to say something to them but she didn't. Walking out of the building,

Corey kissed Alyssa before helping her in her car. He told her to call him as soon as she got home. Watching her drive off, Corey strolled back inside and nodded to Larry as he passed his room.

Thinking of the pain his family was going through, Corey felt that it was time to put Deana to use. It was time for him to help out in some way, shape, or form. Although Tessa and his crew were on the top their list, Corey needed to eliminate Blue and his crew as well. Instead of trying to do shit on his own like before, he was going to let his brothers know about his problem. Even though Blue was only searching for him at the moment, he couldn't help but feel that it was only a matter of time before he found out about Alyssa or anyone else in his family. Corey sent a text to his brothers letting them know he needed to talk to them asap. Finding Deana's name, Corey pushed the call button and waited for her to answer.

"Hey Corey. Wassup?"

"Deana, I need ya help with something important."

9

Drea had to stay in the hospital for two days, and she didn't say shit to Mari the entire time. The shit frustrated the fuck out of him. He knew that he had fucked up and failed to protect her, so he had no choice but to let her have her moment. Mari couldn't lie and say that it wasn't fucking with him because it was. On top of needing to handle the street shit, he had problems at home too and it had his focus a little off. Mari stood to the side of the nurse as she pushed Drea's wheelchair and headed for the exit. She had finally been discharged from the hospital and it was time to go home.

Once they made it to the truck, Mari tried to help Drea get inside, but she snatched away from him. He blew out a frustrated breath, stepped back, and allowed the nurse to help her. After she was secured inside, he walked around to the driver's side and hopped in. The heat was blasting since it was forty-seven degrees outside, but he turned it down since the truck was good and warm. He pulled away from Emory and since the radio wasn't on, silence filled the truck. Mari drove without saying anything until he was completely off of the hospital premises.

"Drea baby... I'm sor..."

"Save your excuses D'Mari Mitchell. Because of your secretive ass, me and my auntie almost lost our fuckin' lives. I've asked you countless times what the hell you had goin' on... the answer was always nothing or you'd blow me off. Well whatever the fuck it is, look where it got us. Headed to *divorce* court," Drea fumed.

"Divorce? Ain't nobody getting a fuckin' divorce ANDREA MITCHELL!!" Mari banged his hand on the steering wheel.

"HOLIDAY!!" she retorted.

Mari bit the inside of his jaw to keep from saying some shit that would make the conversation worse. He continued driving while thinking of how he wanted to say exactly what was on his mind. The fact of the matter was that he was guilty, but Drea was overreacting in his opinion. He figured she would have her day or so of being pissed off, but enough was enough.

"Drea... I'm wrong. I know this, but let's cut the bullshit aight. You a lawyer. You smart as hell, so you know what the deal is without me even saying it. You also know the less you know the better, so we gon' keep it that way. I'll make this shit up to you for the rest of my life, but I can't have you hating me and shit. I need you on my side," Mari expressed.

She didn't even reply to him, but Mari knew that she was digesting what he said. Over the past couple of days, he managed to find an Air BNB out in Alpharetta for the entire family. It was far enough away from all of their houses, but also close enough so that the fellas would be able to handle their business without any interruptions. He knew it was only a matter of time before Drea said anything because he wasn't heading home. A couple of movers had already taken a good bit of their clothes and all of the important shit that they needed. Everyone seemed to be at odds and Mari didn't know if having all of the sisters together under one roof was going to go well for the guys, but there was no way around it.

"Where you goin' D'Mari... this ain't the way home," Drea finally broke the silence.

"Alpharetta," Mari answered, giving the short answer even though he knew that he was going to have to explain himself.

"Alpharetta? What the hell is in Alpharetta? I'm ready to see my babies. Take me home!" Drea demanded.

"The twins are already in Alpharetta. Matter fact, everyone will be. Until we can take care of some shit, we gotta stay together and not go anywhere near our homes."

Mari heard Drea mumble and he saw her rolling her eyes out of the corner of his eye. She leaned back in her seat and closed her eyes, which was fine by him because he was tired of arguing.

An hour later, Mari pulled up to the house and parked around back. His mom's car, amongst a couple others, were there and that meant that Victoria, Aunt Shirley, and the twins were there already too since his mom picked them up. Mari knew seeing the kids would put a smile on Drea's face and he couldn't wait to see it. She was bitter towards him and he only wanted to see her back to herself in some kinda way. Mari hopped out of the truck fast and jogged around and helped Drea out. She tensed up and he could tell that she was still pissed off, but she didn't push him away.

They made their way into the house and Drea's eyes instantly lit up when she laid eyes on DJ and Ava. It was just what Mari expected and what he needed to see.

"Heeyyy mommy's babies... I missed y'all!" Drea went and sat in between her mom and mother-in-law and gave love to the kids.

"Hey daddy's man... hey daddy's princess," Mari pinched both of their cheeks.

The mothers went into the kitchen to start on dinner while Mari stood there staring at his little family in awe. The dream, or nightmare because that's exactly what it was, that he had instantly popped into his head again and a tear threatened to fall from his right eye. He wiped it away, but he could tell that Drea saw it. From the look that she gave him, it let him know that she still loved his ass. Mari told himself that he had to get the street shit together ASAP so that his family could get back to their normal routines.

"Siissstteerrrr!!" Lexi sang as she entered the living room followed by Alyssa and Anastasia.

They all hugged each other and almost instantly, their smiles were gone when they laid eyes on Mari.

"All y'all niggaz got us fucked up," Lexi walked up to him and pointed her finger.

"Aww hell..." he mumbled.

"Alexis sit yo pregnant ass down," J.R.'s voice boomed and she stopped dead in her tracks.

Mari wanted to smirk at how J.R. had her in check, but he had better sense than to do that while in the same room with all of the sisters.

"Aaayyyeee y'all done got the party started," Aunt Shirley's voice could be heard coming from one of the bedrooms that was located down the hall.

"You would think this old ass lady didn't just get shot," Stasia mumbled, but Aunt Shirley's good ass ears heard her.

"I know you ain't thought no lil bullet was gon' change me... I'm Tupac now!!" she stood in the middle of the floor and did a two-step.

Mari couldn't help but to laugh. He was happy that she didn't hate his ass like her nieces.

"I got me a bullet proof vest on the way now tho... y'all lil thugs ain't bout to kill me before my time. I got some more drinking to do," she continued and headed for the kitchen.

"Come let me holla at ya bruh," J.R. motioned for Mari to follow him.

Once they made it downstairs to the basement, J.R. got right down to business. Mari listened to him attentively as he ran down his plan to get at Grant.

"I damn shol' hope this don't backfire bruh," Mari said after J.R. was done talking.

"As long as neither of the sisters find out this part, we'll be good," J.R. assured him.

Mari heard the door creak and walked over and looked out. He didn't see anyone when

HE LOOKED OUT AND HE DAMN SURE HOPED NO ONE HAD heard his and J.R.'s brief conversation.

10

"Aye bae.... Shh....shhh....shhh..."

J.R. stopped in mid stroke to silence Lexi. He knew he had some good dick but she had to be stunting just a little bit, especially with that act she was putting on. Usually, J.R. loved all that loud moaning and screaming, but currently they were fucking in the middle of the day with damn near twenty other people in the crib. He could hear Kyler running and playing outside the door, so he knew they could hear them.

"Fuck themmmmmmmmm..." she moaned out, causing J.R. to start stroking again.

He looked into Lexi's eyes and the way she bit her bottom lip alone had him about to come.

"I'M ABOUT TO CUMMMMM..." SHE SCREAMED OUT, PULLING him as deep as she could inside her without smashing her stomach.

J.R. LEANED IN CLOSER TO LEXI'S FACE AND GRABBED HER bottom lip with his teeth. Not only was that shit sexy, it helped silence her a little bit.

After exploding inside her, he placed one last kiss on her lips before getting up. J.R. headed directly to the connected bathroom and started the shower.

"DAMN, CAN YOU AT LEAST BRING A BITCH A TOWEL?" LEXI screamed as he adjusted the water temperature.

J.R. LET OUT A LOW CHUCKLE BEFORE GRABBING A TOWEL from the small closet. After wetting the towel, he walked halfway in the room and tossed it to her on the bed.

"AYE YO.... YOU RUDE AS FUCK!" SHE CURSED, STICKING UP her middle finger.

ONCE BACK IN THE BATHROOM, J.R JUMPED IN THE SHOWER. After washing up twice, he then grabbed the biggest dry towel, wrapped it around his waist, and left out. Truthfully, he expected Lexi to be sleep but it was no surprise when he discovered her in the middle of the bed, eating chips.

When she noticed him standing there, she looked up and

rolled her eyes before grabbing what he thought was her phone.

"Yo cousin Julian texted you. He wanted to know if you was headed that way yet?" she read.

J.R. shook his head before walking over to the bed and snatching his phone out of her hands.

"Stay out my shit," he warned her with a firm look.

"Boy you on my contract, that's *my* shit," she replied before tossing a Ruffle Cheddar Cheese chip in her mouth.

If it was one thing J.R. learned about being with Alexis Holiday, he learned how to pick his battles. He knew how hotheaded she was and at that very moment, she was looking for any reason to be into it.

Completely ignoring her, he went inside one of the luggage he had yet to unpack and grabbed a pair of Polo draws and Hanes wife beater.

"And where the fuck you meeting Julian at and why? Jeremy, I need you to be careful. I be losing my mind in this house worried about you. We need you baby."

He briefly paused and turned around. When he

locked eyes with Lexi, he could see that she was crying and rubbing her belly. J.R. let out a long sigh before walking over slowly to her and taking a seat on the bed. He carefully thought about what he was going to say before he spoke, which was something he rarely did. He grabbed Lexi and scooted her closer to him, pulling her into a hug.

"I GOT INTO SOME SHIT THAT I SHOULDN'T HAVE, BUT IT'S too fuck'n' late to have regrets," he spoke, pausing momentarily, thinking about Yasmine.

"I CAN'T APOLOGIZE ENOUGH TO YOU BABY. TO YOUR family. To everyone... for putting y'all in this bullshit. I will not lose or damn near lose another person I love," he barked, the first tear escaping his right eye.

HE HEARD LEXI WEEP SOFTLY AND IT ONLY MADE HIM breakdown even more.

"I FUCKED UP...... I FUCKED UP!" HE YELLED, causing her to jump out of his arms.

"LOOK, I'LL BE BACK," HE STATED, STANDING TO HIS FEET and walking back over to the luggage.

J.R. GRABBED A PAIR OF GRAY JOGGING PANTS, AN ALL-white Ralph Lauren Polo t-shit, and socks.

"J.R. where are you going?" she questioned, finally getting out the bed.

J.R. ignored her. He grabbed his wheat Timbs and slipped them on before snatching his Moncler coat.

"So you just gon' fuck'n' ignore me?" she yelled, standing in front of him, blocking his way.

"Lexi, you better get the fuck out my face...."

"Or what Jerrrreeemmmmmyyyyyy," she sang and danced in his face.

J.R. took his hand and rubbed it over his beard while letting out deep breath. He stopped moving and stood in one spot.

"Le-xi..." he said calmly, breaking down her name by the syllable.

He looked down at her as she looked up at him. He stared into her eyes and without saying another word, Lexi moved out of the way. J.R. listened as Lexi huffed, puffed, and cursed under her breath, but he paid her no mind. He was out of the house and in the car before she could blink.

Once in the car, he checked for both guns and shot a text to Julian. Once that text was sent, one came through from Lexi and he regretted reading it.

Big Booty Lexi: You a fuckn clown. Guess I'll prepare for another nigga to raise your baby cuz you either gon be dead or in jail (middle finger emoji)

Lexi's text caused him to buss a U-Turn in the middle of the street. He was tired of playing with her, but she was gon' learn to respect him after today. J.R. made it to the light right before the Air BNB and turned right. Dealing with Lexi and any relationship bullshit was only going to distract him from what mattered, so he had to stay focused.

J.R. hadn't been back to Tracey's bar since the shooting, but he was cool with the owner Trigga; he knew it wasn't an issue. As soon as he pulled into the lot, he spotted the back of Julian's head before it disappeared behind the door.

"Just in time," he mumbled to himself before exiting his car and entering the bar.

"What up you fat fuck?" J.R. said, causing Julian to turn around as the waitress led him to a table near the back.

"You on time huh?" Julian replied once J.R. caught up to him.

The two cousins embraced in a manly hug before taking a seat.

"So, what's been up? How you holding up?" Julian broke the ice and asked.

"Shid, as to be expected, I guess. What you wanted to meet about?" J.R. replied, cutting right to the chase.

"I want you to meet somebody," he smirked, picking up the menu.

"Who?" he quizzed.

Before Julian could reply, a woman appeared out of nowhere and stood on the side of their table.

J.R. looked up slowly, like they did in the movies, from her thick thighs all the way to her flawless face. He had met some bad bitches in life but shorty he was staring at was by far THEE baddest.

"J.R., this my homie Kellz. Kellz, this my cousin J.R." Julian said, introducing the two.

Kellz looked down at J.R., who sat there mesmerized, and spoke.

"Hey how you doing?" she said, licking her lips, making J.R.'s dick harder than Chinese Algebra.

11

D'Mani's decision to give Anastasia space had not been an easy one. In fact, it had been one of the hardest things he'd ever had to do and that was saying a lot. Well, that was until his brother had come up with the idea for everyone to live in the same house to ensure the family's safety. The other side of a massive mansion was not what he had in mind when he thought about giving Stasia space. Out of sight and out of mind had been the goal, but with the two of them under the same roof, regardless of how big, he knew he would run into her eventually. And that was what he was dreading.

With all of the changes that had taken place, he had yet to talk to Cheyanne about whatever she meant in the message she'd left him. The way it sounded, it was bad news and as childish as it was, he wasn't trying to hear about no more bad shit. Not anytime soon anyway. So, when he'd gone to drop Imani back off, he acted as if he didn't have time to stay. He wasn't ready to deal with the possibility of her being pregnant. At the time, the effects of running up in Cheyanne raw hadn't been on his mind. While he could blame it on not having gotten any in a while or even Anastasia having that nigga in his house, he knew that it was just poor judgment on his part.

D'Mani stepped out of his room in a black Nike hoodie, black Prada jeans, and some black ACG boots. He didn't have a clue what the day was going to bring, but he was more than prepared for the bullshit, as long as it wasn't under the same roof as Stasia. The only good thing about living there was the fact that he was able to see Kyler now, and it wasn't shit she could do about it. Although, between checking the traps, avoiding Stasia, and trying to get at Tessa and their other enemies, they hadn't really been able to kick it how they used to. He hoped they would be able to get shit handled soon though so that they could. He missed little man.

D'Mani descended the stairs and headed to the kitchen to grab something to eat before leaving out the house and immediately regretted it. Anastasia sat at the table eating her usual breakfast as of late, some oatmeal with strawberries. As soon as she heard his heavy footsteps, she looked up and gave him a stank ass face. He watched silently as she stood up and went to empty her bowl even though it looked as if she hadn't eaten much.

"You bouta throw away yo whole breakfast just cause I came in the kitchen?" he questioned, unamused by her theatrics.

"What can I say? The sight of you made me lose my appetite." She finished dumping her plate and then gave him a sarcastic smirk. D'Mani let his eyes roam her body, noting how thick she looked in the pink and white Adidas leggings and matching crop top. It'd been a minute since he'd felt the softness of her walls, and he could only imagine how fire that shit would be after going without it for so long.

"Stop flexin' Anastasia, you know you fuckin' miss me." Just that fast, he was ready to forget the shit he'd been saying about space. It was always harder to ignore his love for her when she was in his presence. He'd been all set to be business as usual until he set eyes on. her, and now it wasn't no way that he could walk out of there without trying to resolve their issues.

"I do, I really fuckin' do, but do you think that an apology is enough! I been told you it was some bullshit in the water, but yo ass didn't wanna hear it. Now after you did exactly what I was afraid of, you think I'm sposed to just let it go, cause I miss you?" she scrunched her face like what he was saying was the dumbest shit she'd ever heard, and when she said it like that, he had to admit that she had a point. Since there was so much shit going on, he hadn't been able to woo her like he should have, but that didn't take away from the fact that he did love and miss her something terrible. D'Mani released a heavy sigh and moved closer to her, hoping that she let him. When she stayed in the same spot, he continued his advance until he was close enough to pull her into his arms.

"I more than understand what you sayin' ma, but if this week ain't taught us nothin' else, haven't we learned that life's too short? If you need to hear a nigga say *sorry* a million times a day, I will... that shit was a mistake, and I knew that as soon as it was over. If anything, it made me realize how much I love and want to be with you. I know I can't take it back, but I'll spend the rest of my life making that shit up to you." He pleaded and meant that shit from the bottom of his heart. If he had to prove his love every day, he was willing to. Anastasia was *it* for him and he couldn't see himself without her, that was for damn sure.

He could see that she was struggling with forgiving him; it was written all over her face. Figuring that he would give her some help with her decision, he hastily pressed his lips against hers. She put up a small fight at first but eventually, she melted into him and let his tongue explore her mouth.

D'Mani held her tighter, trying to put all of his feelings for her into that one kiss, and his efforts seemed to be working as she let out a low moan. Their physical attraction and steamy sex had always been a big part of their relationship and although she probably hated him right then, that wasn't something she could deny.

In no time, he had her wedged between him and the counter, pressing his erection into her center and roaming her body with his hands. He released her lips long enough to plant a few wet kisses on her neck as he slipped his hand into her leggings, and that's when it seemed like her senses returned because she gave his chest a light shove.

"No, D'Mani." He continued his assault on her body though, feeling as if he could recapture the moment.

"Stasia you know this shit feels right! That's because *we* feel right." He pleaded, looking deep into her eyes, but already, he could tell that the small window of opportunity he had was gone and her pain had returned.

"I can't.....every time I look at you, every time you touch me, I'm right back in the kitchen seeing you touch her the same way and ... I just can't deal with that shit right now!" her voice cracked as tears threatened to fall. Before he could even say anything back, she was running away from him and out of the kitchen.

"Fuck!" D'Mani cursed. He was so close to getting through to her. The fact that she was showing more hurt than anger had let him know that her walls were breaking down for him. He just needed to try harder, space was definitely out of the question.

D'Mani looked up in time to see Alyssa walking into the kitchen and immediately turned around to leave at the sight of him.

"Aye Lyssa hold up!" he called out and rushed to stop her before she got too far away. He caught her right around the corner since pregnancy stopped her from being able to move as fast as she wanted.

"What?" she hissed, swatting at the hand that he had on her arm. "If my sister not fuckin' with you, then I ain't either." He stopped himself from chuckling at her as she stood there with her arms folded over her belly and her lip poked out.

"I know, I know." He held his hands up in surrender and her eyes softened. "I just wanted to know if you could give me some advice you know... to get back in her good graces." It was weird as hell having to ask for help when it came to his woman, but he was willing to do whatever he needed to, and if that meant enlisting her sister then so be it. She seemed to think on it for a second before she smirked.

"And what do I get out of helping you?" she cocked her head to the side and asked. "I'm risking my sister being mad at me for even talkin' to you let alone helping yo cheating ass." D'Mani racked his brain thinking of what he could offer up for her help and a slow smile crept onto his face.

"What if I promised you whatever snack yo lil pregnant heart wanted... whenever you wanted?" He added once he saw her about to object. He knew that females had all types of weird ass cravings at odd hours and since Corey was jammed up, he figured he could help her out with that, especially since the women were basically on lock down until shit got handled.

"You tryna call me fat?" she hissed instantly, making D'Mani's smile slip.

"No. No!" he grabbed her arm again, stopping her from storming off. "I'm just sayin I can help you out when you have a taste for something that ain't in the crib," he pleaded.

"Whenever I want?" she narrowed her eyes and pointed at him.

"Whenever you want, day or night."

"Fine! You gotta deal." She stuck her hand out so they could shake on it and D'Mani quickly accepted. "Now first piece of advice, diamonds are always a good start. And I want some Snickers ice cream when you bring yo cheatin' ass back!" she huffed, walking away and this time he let her.

D'Mani sighed in relief; at least he had one sister willing to help him even though he'd had to bribe her. Now all he had to do was fit a trip to the jewelry store into his day. He just hoped that this time she actually accepted that shit. Heading to the door, he paused as his phone went off. He started not to answer since he didn't recognize the number but decided it could be an emergency, so he hurried and slid the green icon across the screen.

"Hello?"

"Hi, this is nurse Johnson from Piedmont Hospital, I'm calling for a D'Mani."

"That's me!" D'Mani cut her off instantly, panicking at the thought of something being wrong with his daughter.

"Well umm, we have Cheyanne Smith here, she was rushed into emergency with her daughter and you're listed as an emergency contact," she informed him.

"Rushed to the hospital? What's wrong with her, is she okay?"

"Actually I don't really have much information at this time. I'm really only calling because your daughter is here alone."

D'Mani didn't even let her finish her sentence before he hung up and rushed out of the house. A million thoughts ran through his mind as he jumped into his truck and high tailed it out of the gates; the main one being *what the hell was wrong with Cheyanne?*

12

As the weeks passed, Corey kept to his regular routine at the rehab. He attended group meetings regularly and continued to show improvement. Although Corey started out attending the meetings so he could get back to his family quicker, he didn't think that his attendance in the group rap sessions would actually pay off. Dr. Fields, his psychologist, praised the progress Corey was making and informed him that she would be having a discussion with the administration about his release. That shit was like music to his ears and he couldn't wait to share the news with his family. Although things were going were going well for him, he had yet to unlock the mystery behind the connection between Larry, Janice and Larry's sister. Corey had been keeping his eyes and ears opened and he had Deana on her toes as well. He had her making moves on the outside as well as in the rehab. She reported everything, even the irrelevant shit to Corey about Blue and whatever Janice was up. The information that Deana had given him wasn't useful but he appreciated her effort.

After his last visit with Alyssa, she updated him about

the family's new living arrangements in Alpharetta and how his brothers had her and his sister-in-laws on lock down. Corey couldn't help but laugh at his wife's frustration, but he explained to her that it was for their own good. Lyssa wasn't trying to hear that shit, but she knew as well as he did that there was no sense in arguing about it. When Alyssa mentioned that they were decorating the house for Christmas, Corey realized then that the joyous holiday was less than a week away. His wife cooed as she informed him that he was able to come home for Christmas Day. Corey didn't want to kill her excitement but spending time with his family was the last thing on his mind; but to make his wife happy, Corey braced himself for another holiday with his family.

When Mani came to get him on Christmas morning, Corey was more than happy to see his brother. As they headed to the mansion, his brother filled him in on the latest drama with him and Stasia. Corey just shook when Mani told him about his moment of passion with his baby mama and how Stasia caught them in the act. Mani informed Corey that he had to bribe Alyssa with food in order for her to help him win her back, causing him to go into a fit a laughter. The fact that his brother had to make late night trips to the store for Alyssa fucked with Corey a little bit, but he appreciated his cousin for what he was doing and thanked him.

They arrived at the mansion an hour and some change later and Corey nodded his head in approval. Before they got into the house, the door swung open and Alyssa pushed Mani out the way and smothered Corey with kisses. The way she kissed him let him know that she was horny and wanted sex, and he wasn't about to deny his wife of something that they both needed. Alyssa led the way to her room, ignoring the remarks that their family made about them being nasty. As soon as they were behind closed doors, Corey removed her pajamas, laid Alyssa on her side, slid inside her tight wet walls, and enjoyed what he missed for the past two months.

After their hour of love making, they freshened up and joined the rest of the family downstairs. While Alyssa dipped off into the kitchen with the rest of the women, Corey joined the men in the basement/man cave where they were playing *NBA 2K19* on the PS4. His brothers filled him in on what was going on with Tessa and the moves that they were making to track down his cartel. Corey just nodded his head as he listened to J.R. lay out the plan he was putting in motion. Mari updated him on how the business was doing and how nothing was stopping their cash flow, which was always good to hear. When Kyler called them for dinner, Mari pulled Corey to the side, inquiring about him *not* returning to rehab and staying at the house since he seemed to be doing better, especially since Alyssa would be giving birth any day. Corey truly wanted to accept his offer, but he declined saying that he felt like he needed to stay there a little while longer. His brother gave him the side eye but respected his wishes.

During family dinner, Corey informed the family that his release date from rehab was soon approaching and everyone seemed genuinely happy for him. He expected some jokes to be made about him being a crackhead or how he better not relapse but they never came. Even though they were all happy to be spending the holiday together, Christmas wasn't as joyous as it should have been. With the twins at odds with their women and J.R. dealing with the possibility that his sister was dead, no one really seemed to be enjoying the holiday except for the kids. However, Aunt Shirley provided enough entertainment to keep everyone smiling, laughing, and in good spirits.

When it was time for him to return to the rehab, everyone was either too drunk or high too drive, so he took an Uber back. Corey promised to call Alyssa as soon as he got there before getting in the car. He arrived at rehab an hour later, tipping the driver before he got out. Corey was about to head inside until Deana called him over to her car. With her phone in hand, she showed him a picture of man that she confirmed was Blue and where he was spotted at. She gave Corey all the tea on where he hangs at, how much time he spends there, and how many henchman he had. Without hesitation, Corey reached in his pocket, peeled off ten C-notes, and handed them to Deana but she refused to accept the money. Instead of arguing with her, he placed the money in her pursed, thanked her, and headed inside. Bumping into Larry's sister, they locked eyes for a moment and the stare down she gave him was intense, and the look of disgust that was displayed on her face made him give her the same one in return. The light-skinned woman looked familiar to him. Like he saw her at one of places he used to gamble at or near one of the trap houses, but he couldn't recall where. Larry caught them in the awkward moment and before he could ask any questions, Corey strolled down the hall to his room. He knew he was going to have a few more sleepless nights as he put a plan in motion to take out Blue.

The ringing of his cell interrupted Corey's workout. Judging how it was five in the morning, he knew nobody was timing him that early except his wife. Corey snatched his phone off the bed and answered.

"Happy New Year's Eve, bae!" she beamed.

"Happy New Year's Eve, Lyssa," he chuckled. "Why are you up so early?"

"I couldn't sleep due to the baby. She's very active this morning for some reason."

"Because it's almost that time for her to enter the world. That's probably her way of letting you know that she might be coming today," he joked.

"Don't play. This baby not supposed to be here til' next week."

"Just in case she decides to come early, you better get everything together, just to be on the safe side. Aight?"

"Aight," she rolled her eyes.

The couple discussed baby names for the first time since discovering that she was pregnant and Alyssa disapproved all the ratchet names that her husband came up with for their child. When they finally decided on a name, it was after seven in the morning. Corey was enjoying the conversation he was having with his wife. Talking to her seemed to always cause him to forget about his problems and put him in a better place; but when he saw Larry standing in the doorway of his room, Corey was instantly brought back to reality of where he was. After coming up with an excuse to end the call, he told his wife he loved her then hung up.

"Wassup man?" Corey sat on the edge of his bed.

"That what I'm tryna figure out my nigga," Larry stepped in, closing the door.

Corey knew exactly what Larry was referring to. Since coming across his sister on Christmas night, he'd been avoiding Larry the past few days and whenever they did speak, Corey was brief. Not saying more than few words to him before going to his room where he spent most of his time.

"Look, I've just been trying to stay out the way and think of my next move with this nigga Blue," he halfway lied.

"We'll get to that nigga in a minute. I need to know wassup with you and Izzy," Larry folded his arms across his chest.

Corey scrunched his face as to say *who the fuck is that*.

"My sister nigga."

"Ain't shit up with us. She just looked familiar to me. That's all."

"So y'all ain't got no type of history or any bad blood between y'all? Because the way y'all motherfuckas were staring each other down the other night looked like y'all were about to throw bows."

"She gave me the look of disgust as soon as she saw me. So, I returned it. I never exchanged words with shawty or none of that. So, I don't know why she gave me the attitude," Corey shrugged.

"I ain't even gonna hold you. She has been more bitchy than usual and a reliable source informed me that she be hanging with that bitch Janice in the streets," he shook his head.

"I wanted to ask you about that because I saw your sister and Janice chopping it up in the stairway a while back. I don't know if she saw you that day or not. I'm not sure, but I think ya sister be up here to see Janice more than she comes to see you."

Corey could tell that his words had gotten to Larry by the way his eyebrows raised. Since the time was approaching for him to make his move on Blue, he figured he needed to find out if Larry was really a friend or enemy. Although Corey wanted to believe that he was on his side, he couldn't afford to take any chances.

"You think the two of them might be up to something?" Larry questioned.

"I don't know, but I think Janice's sneaky ass might be working with or for one my other enemies. Something popped off with my folks a few weeks back and she knew about the shit before I did," Corey tried to conceal his anger.

Larry nodded his head in silence as he shifted his eyes to the floor as if he was thinking about something. Corey watched him for a few seconds as thoughts of his own entered his head.

"If this nigga know who the fuck hit up my family or played a part in it, I'm gonna kill this motherfucka."

"So, what did you want to tell me about Blue," Corey broke their moment of silence.

"I got info about the spot he's gonna be at tonight and picture of what the nigga look like. So, if you wanna ride out tonight, we can," Larry said, rubbing his hands together like Birdman.

"We?"

"Yeah, *we* nigga. You think I've been getting all this info just to sit on the sideline? Fuck that! I want in. Plus it's been a minute since I got my hands dirty anyway," he smirked. "So, are we rolling or nah?"

Corey took a moment to think things over. He was uncomfortable as fuck with the idea of rolling with Larry to handle this nigga simply because he only moved solo or with his brothers. Even though they were cool, Corey didn't know how Larry moved or what he was like in the streets. At the moment, it seemed like Larry had the upper hand on him because he had more information on Corey than he had on Larry. Not wanting to miss the opportunity to handle this shit, he decided to roll with Larry, despite his doubts.

"Aight. I'm in."

The two men shook hands and Larry informed him that he would take care of the escape route throughout the day and let him know what time they were moving out. Corey nodded his head in understanding and finished the rest of his workout when Larry exited his room.

As the day went on, Corey chilled in his room, getting his mind right about what he was going to that night. The more he thought about rolling with Larry to take out Blue, the more he wanted to change his mind and handle the shit on his own; but since he wanted to get the shit over and done with, Corey continued to push those nagging feelings to the back of his mind. Around nine that evening, Larry told him that they were moving out at ten and Corey was more than ready to go. The trap music he was listening to had him on ten and he was ready to put that work in. The thought of him killing again had him at odds with himself. When he ran down on Lou and his crew, Corey was high and drunk out of his mind and couldn't recall what he done the next day. The alcohol and pills that were in his system was the influence behind his actions but now that he didn't need the alcohol or the drugs, he wondered why his urge to kill had kicked back in with ease. The positive side of things was that Corey was well aware of what he was about to do. Nothing influenced his actions but the need to protect himself and his family and that was all the motivation he needed to pull the trigger.

At ten on the nose, Larry and Corey dipped into the stairway, jogged down the , and headed out the back door. They ran down the half lit alley way across the street to a black moving van with tinted windows. Unlocking the doors, Larry hopped behind the wheel and Corey hopped in the passenger's seat. He observed the van and when he saw that they were alone, he let out a sigh of relief. Corey noticed the jumpsuits, ski masks, and guns placed in the back of the van before Larry pulled off into traffic, making his way to 285. Fifteen minutes into the ride, he felt his phone vibrate in his pocket. He saw it was Alyssa and let the phone go straight to voicemail. He did that for the next three calls, but when she called a fifth time, Corey answered.

"Baby, what's wrong?"

"This Stasia! You need to get ya ass to the hospital now. Lyssa about to have the baby!"

"Fuck! Aight! Text me the address!"

"I already sent it. Get here now!"

Corey went to his text messages and put the address in his Google maps.

"Wassup?"

"I need you to take me to WellStar North Fulton Hospital in Alpharetta. My wife about to give birth to my daughter," he smiled.

Without hesitation, Larry put the pedal to the medal, heading towards Alpharetta. Corey was glad that the cops weren't lurking on the highway like they usually were because they would've gotten pulled over for sure. Corey's heart was beating out of his chest and hands began to sweat. Although he knew the day was coming, he wasn't prepared for the birth of his baby girl. At one point, Corey didn't even think he was fit to be a father because of the shit he was involved in, plus his drug and alcohol addiction. He feared that he wouldn't be able to live up to his own expectations of himself, let alone the expectations of Alyssa's when it came to him being a father. But since he was on the straight and narrow, Corey was ready to be the man he should've been from the start.

Coming to an abrupt stop in the emergency parking lot, Corey shook Larry's hand before getting out the car. Running into the emergency, he stopped at the nurse's station to ask about his wife, but when Drea called his name, he walked over to her and she took him to where Alyssa was.

"You got here just in time. They had her in there for fifteen minutes and all she keep screaming is that she's not pushing out nothing until her husband gets here," Drea informed him.

Corey chuckled as they powered walked to the operating room.

"Bout time ya ass got here. Now get in there so my sister can have this baby," Lexi pointed to the operating room.

Pushing the doors open, Corey saw the doctors were gathered around her and Victoria was by her side. Alyssa was fighting with the nurses who were trying to get her to calm down.

"Baby... baby... stop fighting... I'm here now. Okay? I'm here now," he rushed to the other side of her, kissing her forehead.

"I knew you were going to make it," Alyssa gave an exhausted smile.

"Okay, Alyssa. Your husband is here. Are you ready to have this baby now?" the doctor asked.

"Yeah. I'm ready."

"Okay. I need you to give me a big push."

Gripping Corey and Victoria's hands, Alyssa did as the doctor instructed. After three pushes, Alyssa was ready to throw in the towel, but Corey encouraged her to give it one more push. After the next push, they heard the cry of their daughter. They smiled as they watched the doctor cut the umbilical cord and washed the baby off. A few minutes later, the nurse handed the baby to Alyssa and they instantly fell in love with their six-pound, seven-ounce baby girl Alana Chloe Washington.

Corey placed another kiss on Alyssa's forehead before kissing their daughter's forehead. Victoria cried tears of joy as she watched her daughter and son-in-law with their new baby. Corey had no idea that something so small and adorable could have him wrapped around his finger already and she was only few minutes old. As he continued to stare at his daughter in awe, returning to the rehab center was out of the question. All of the shit he had going on had to take the back seat for a minute. His wife and daughter needed him and nothing was going to take him away from them. Nothing.

13

Christmas had come and gone, and the New Year was only hours away. Things between Mari and Drea were still sketchy, but they were surviving. Even though she only said the bare minimum to him, Mari was glad that she hadn't brought up the word *'divorce'* again. She didn't listen to him about not working, so Mari was sure to have security detail follow her at all times. Actually, all of the couples were at odds, but the men still had them protected no matter what. The thought of *losing* their women was too much to even think of. Mari's heart went out to his boy J.R. because he had lost so much in so little time. Even though they hadn't found Yasmine, everyone knew the chances of finding her alive were slim to none.

Mari planned on bringing the New Year in at home with his family so that's why he was out taking care of business that day. He noticed the sour look that Drea gave him right before he left at nine that morning, but he planned on making it up to her. Three business meetings later, Mari finally pulled up to the warehouse that was out near Buckhead a little after six o'clock. The business that he had to conduct had to be done at night time, but if everything ran smooth, he would be back to the place they had been calling home by ten or so. After parking around back, the truck that he was waiting for turned onto the street and Mari got out and went inside through the side door. He let the garage up and the eighteen-wheeler backed in shortly afterwards. All three of the men got out and then got down to business.

He looked on as the guys made trip after trip, taking the shipments inside. The process that they had put in place had been running so smooth that it was about to time to double everything once again. With everything that was going on in the streets, it confirmed that they all needed to be in and out in a few years. Once that truck left, the next one pulled in right on schedule and it was the one that Mari was really waiting on. Duffle bag after duffel bag after duffle bag was transported to his office and he got right down to business. They never had the money and drugs on the same truck for safety precautions.

After running the money through the machine four times, the count was still off by ten grand. Ten grand was chump change to what they were bringing in, but it was *too much* to let it go unknown. There had never been any money problems. Not if you don't count Corey's mishaps, but all of the workers had been thorough as fuck. Mari shot a text to the Rock Boyz to let them know what was going on. He hoped that it was an honest mistake because if not, that was another problem that was going to be added to their long list of shit. Instead of questioning any of the workers, Mari decided that it was best to sit back and watch how everything played out. His phone rang and when he noticed that it was his bruh, he picked up right away.

"What it do bruh? You still goin' through wit that shit?"

"Hell yeah! Gotta do what I gotta do to get shit poppin' man," J.R. responded.

Mari sighed, but he understood the position that they were in. It didn't help that he felt like some shit was going to go wrong, but he prayed his feelings were wrong.

"I feel you, I feel you. Just hurry up and get it over wit. We got enough got damn problems," Mari expressed.

They chopped it up for a few more minutes. After he secured the money in the floor safe, he headed out. Mari sent Drea a text letting her know that he was on the way. She left him on read and he shook his head. It wasn't that he was surprised, but he just hoped that with the New Year about to roll in that Drea would get back to herself. Mari stopped and picked up the orders that he had placed that consisted of Drea's favorites things and made his way home. It was a little after nine when he made it back. He was going to have to make two trips to retrieve everything, but that was cool. As long as it put a smile on his wife's face, that was all that mattered.

Mari walked in and was shocked that no one was in the living room. An eerie feeling came over him and he dropped everything that was in his hands and grabbed his gun from his waist, turning off the safety. He walked slowly towards the kitchen and the nanny turned around and screamed when she saw the gun in his hand.

"Where everybody at?" Mari quizzed and relaxed a little once she relaxed.

"The babies are sleeping. Everyone else is at the hospital... WellStar North. I thought Mrs. Andrea called..."

Mari didn't give her a chance to finish her sentence before he was out the door. So many thoughts were running through his mind as he made the drive to the hospital. Anger was setting in because Drea didn't even call him. To add to that, he had texted her ass and she read it but didn't reply. She had taken her level of being pissed off to a whole nother level. Mari didn't know what could have happened to cause all of the family to be at the hospital, but he was about to find out shortly. He found a parking spot right near the entrance, whipped into it, killed the engine, and hopped out. As soon as he entered the doors, he came face to face with Lexi walking out of the door with a scowl on her face and her phone in her hand.

"I'm gon' kill yo boy as soon as I see his ass," she fumed and Mari knew that J.R. had fucked up royally.

14

J.R. grabbed the greasy bag from the woman at the drive-thru window at Cook Out and sped off. He had a full day ahead of him, but he first had to feed Jessica. Things with her had took a drastic turn. He went from shooting her in both legs and knocking her teeth out to aiding her back to health. For the past couple of weeks, J.R. made sure she was straight and for that, she was helping him bring down the Tessa Cartel, one brother at a time.

"J.R., I said Sprite, this lemonade." Jessica complained, turning up her nose as she took a sip.

Although Jessica was in a good position with J.R, he still didn't trust her fully, that's why he had workers watching her around the clock. Being a man of his word, if everything worked out in their favor then she'd be set free.

"Look, you better drink that shit," he finally replied, pulling his onion rings from her bag.

"So, how's operation Elliot coming along?" she quizzed before stuffing her mouth with a handful of fries.

"I gotta go holler at Julian about that right now. That's why I'm finna bounce," he replied, standing to his feet.

"Thanks for the food and remember what I told you." She schooled him before he made his exit.

As soon as J.R. foot hit the first step, his phone rang. He pulled it from his pocket, peeped it was Lexi calling, and silenced it. Ever since she said that slick shit about another man raising his child, J.R. had barely said two words to his girl. Lexi was just as stubborn as him, so the both of them walked around each day, not even acknowledging each other's presence. Usually J.R. wasn't with the childish shit but his attention was elsewhere, which made it even easier to ignore her.

"I'll be back later. D'Mari will be stopping by to drop off that work. Resse, make sure you lock up. I'll holler at you niggas later." J.R. stated before exiting the trap house.

Jumping into the car, he wasted no time peeling off into traffic, heading to his next meeting. Fifteen minutes later, J.R. was pulling inside the parking lot of Bones Restaurant, a little steakhouse joint him and Lexi visited frequently.

He was meeting both Julian and Kellz there but after scanning the parking lot, Julian car was nowhere to be found. Figuring his cousin was late as usual, J.R. checked his surrounding, secured his piece, and got out the vehicle.

Walking inside, the place was packed; luckily for him, he was a regular so when the hostesses Tammy spotted him, she snatched up two menus and greeted him.

"Where's big belly? She's not joining us today?" she asked, referring to Lexi.

"Nah, I'm waiting on my cousin," he laughed, thinking about how big Lexi had actually gotten.

"Oh ok. Right this way."

Just as J.R. started to follow her, he heard a woman call his name. Slowly turning around, he spotted Kellz walking towards him in a pair of tight ripped up jeans and heels. From where he was standing, he couldn't help but to admire her body. Kellz was the true definition of thick, flat ass, big stomach, and small waist.

Thanking the hostess, he waited for Kellz to reach the table before he took a seat.

"Nice seeing you again," she smiled.

"Same to you," he replied nonchalantly.

"Where the fuck is Julian?" he questioned, looking around the restaurant.

"Oh, wait. He ain't text you? He told me that he had to take care of some business and for me to fill him in later. So, it looks like it'll just be me and you," she smirked.

J.R. WAS TRYING TO FIGURE OUT IF HE WAS TWEAKING OR was she indeed flirting with him; either way, he wanted no parts.

"AIGHT COOL, SO HOW MUCH HAS JULIAN ACTUALLY TOLD you?" he questioned, flipping through the pages of the menu.

"NOT MUCH HONESTLY. HE TOLD ME THAT YOU WOULD GET into more details. He pretty much asked for my help and here I am," she explained, tossing her hands in the air.

"YOU AGREED QUICK AS FUCK TO NOT KNOW MUCH," J.R. looked up and stated, trying to see if it was something he was missing.

"TWO YEARS AGO, I CAUGHT A BODY AND LET'S JUST SAY, I owe your cousin with my life. It's a long story but...."

"NAH, SAY LESS. YOU GOOD," HE INSURED HER, SECRETLY wanting to know more about it but he played it cool.

"OK, SO LOOK RIGHT….."

J.R. SPENT AN HOUR EXPLAINING THINGS TO KELLZ WHO listened attentively. He ran down everything to her, sometimes telling her things that was against his better judgment, but he had no choice. He had to trust her, whether he knew her or not. He did the same thing with D'Mani, D'Mari, and Corey and they had yet to make him regret it. He trusted his cousin Julian with his life, so he knew if he co-signed for Kellz, she had to be straight.

"CAN I GET YOU GUYS A SHOT BEFORE I GRAB THAT BILL?" Their waitress appeared out of nowhere and asked.

"NAH, I'M GOOD," KELLZ QUICKLY TURNED IT DOWN.

HE WASN'T SURE IF IT WAS HER HEAVY BALTIMORE ACCENT or the way her light brown eyes slanted when she smiled, but he had never been so mesmerized.

"AND YOU SIR?" SHE TURNED TO J.R. AND ASKED.

"YEAH, LET ME GET TWO DOUBLE SHOTS OF PATRON," HE requested, noticing the look on 's face.

"WHAT?" HE CHUCKLED.

"TWOOOOOOOOOOO!" SHE JOKED, MIMICKING Soulja Boy and his social media meme.

J.R. COULDN'T HELP BUT LAUGH. HE HAD NO IDEA SHE could be goofy since she was so serious during their conversation.

"ONE IS FOR YOU," HE REPLIED, GRABBING ONE SHOT OUT of the waitress hand and handing it to her.

"Thank you ma'am," he said in his next breath, grabbing his shot.

ONCE THE WAITRESS WAS GONE, KELLZ SLID THE SHOT glass back over to him.

"THIS IS TECHNICALLY A BUSINESS MEETING AND….." SHE began to decline but he silenced her.

"MAN, SHUT THE FUCK UP AND DRINK!" HE ORDERED, tossing his glass back while Kellz quickly followed suit.

THE TWO OF THEM TALKED FOR ANOTHER HOUR AND before they knew it, they were four rounds in. Realizing that he still had shit to do and being drunk wasn't on the agenda, he stopped.

"I'll go ahead and call my Uber," Kellz said, grabbing her phone after noticing J.R. looking at his watch.

"Uber? Fuck you in an Uber for?" he asked, going into his pocket and tossing bills on the table.

"Wellll... you know I'm not from here and Julian been driving me around. He was busy so I took an Uber," she explained.

"Yo hotel only down the street, I'll take you," he remembered her saying.

J.R. got up slowly from the booth and put his coat on.

"You sure?" she asked, looking up at him and smiling.

"Come on." He motioned with his head as he headed to the exit.

He heard her heels clicking on the floor and he knew she agreed. Once at the door, he held it open for her. Half of him was being a gentleman while the other half wanted to see her ass. He had never been so happy to park so far away in his life. He watched her booty bounce up and down until she reached the door. J.R. then hit the alarm so she could get in. Once the both of them was situated, he peeled off.

Connecting his Bluetooth between his phone and car, he put on some Blac Youngsta and rapped along while he headed up the street to her hotel. Noticing Kellz reciting every word with him, he reached to turn the knob up but mistakenly answered an incoming call for Lexi, just as Kellz spoke.

"THE HOTEL RIGHT HERE."

KELLZ POINTED OUT THE WINDOW WHILE J.R. MADE AN unexpected right. The sound of Lexi's voice blasting through the speakers damn near caused him to crash.

"BITCH I KNOW YOU FUCKING LYING!!" SHE screamed while J.R. tried to control the wheel.

JUST AS HE WAS ABOUT TO REPLY, HIS PHONE DIED.

15

Cheyanne was dying. D'Mani couldn't get that thought out of his head. It was hard for him to believe that the mother of his only child had been carrying around that fatal secret the whole time that she'd been back. He wanted to be mad at her for not saying anything the whole time and ultimately putting his daughter at risk by living with her alone, but the girl was literally on her deathbed.

When the doctor told him about her condition and how she'd had a heart attack while only her and their daughter were home, D'Mani's first reaction was shock and then anger immediately followed. Had it not been for Imani knowing how to call 911 in emergencies, there was no telling what could have happened; but once he got to her room and saw her with tubes and IV's all over, he couldn't bring himself to do shit but hold her hand. Cheyanne didn't have one family member that she could call on, and he figured the last thing she needed after a near death experience was him coming down on her head for not telling him about it.

Days later and he was still fucked up about the whole

thing, trying to figure out a way to tell Imani about what was happening to her mother. All she'd been told so far was that she was sick, and in her small mind, she thought that it was just something like a cold. Imani thought her mama would be okay soon, and D'Mani didn't want to be the one to tell her that she wasn't going to be.

He'd used his schedule of monitoring the traps, catering to Stasia, and stuffing Alyssa with snacks to take his mind off of the inevitable because every time he looked at his daughter, he was reminded of the fact that she would soon be motherless. The doctor told him that Cheyanne's heart was failing and she had mere months to live if he could guess. D'Mani still hadn't even told anyone, not even his mama, but soon he would have to come up off that piece of information and he knew it. Even though he felt bad about her condition, D'Mani couldn't help but feel a small bit of relief at the fact that she wasn't pregnant or claiming to be anyway. Since his talk with Alyssa, he worked out the best way to get back in Anastasia's good graces and an outside baby would definitely ruin his chances of doing so.

Stasia had just started talking to him without saying some smart shit and he had to say that he owed a lot of that to Alyssa. Mani really should have enlisted her help sooner because basically she told him exactly what Stasia was saying about the situation. So far, he'd been pretty consistent in his attempts to win her over and it seemed to be working; but he was expecting to take her out with what he had planned next.

With the help of Alyssa, he'd sent her out to a full day of pampering as soon as she woke up at the Waldorf Astoria, where she was gonna get the full service of a massage, facial, or whatever else females be getting at them places. Next, he had booked her an appointment to get her hair and makeup done and then her nails. He even ordered lunch for her while she was at the hair salon, and he knew that when she got home and saw the long, black low cut Versace dress and red bottoms that he had gotten his stylist to put together, she was going to be excited.

It had been a while since he had been able to do some romantic shit for her, and despite how fucked up in the head he was about Cheyanne being sick, he planned to push that shit to the back of his mind while he catered to his woman.

D'Mani left out of the trap after picking up the week's take. He smirked as his phone buzzed, showing an incoming call from Anastasia. He knew her mean ass was going to call him once Alyssa told her what he had planned for her.

"What's up ma?" he cheesed, dropping the bag he carried into the trunk and sliding into the driver's seat.

"Don't *what's up ma* me nigga! What yo sneaky ass got goin' on?" he could hear the smile in her voice, despite her trying to sound all tough and shit. The time on his dash said that it was barely after one, so he knew that she was at the hair salon already and had just received her food.

"I ain't got shit goin' on woman, just tryna do somethin' special for you. Did you get your food already?" D'Mani asked anxiously. He had ordered the Main Squeeze platter for her and Alyssa's greedy ass since that was her favorite thing to eat from the Punch Bowl. She let out something like a moan and came back on the line.

"Mmmm! Hell yeah I got it! You know I love lobster rolls!" He could almost picture the look of pleasure on her face as she talked to him with her mouth full.

"Can I get a *thank you* with yo hungry ass?"

"Ugh... thank you...I guess, but it's gone take more than my favorite food to get back on my good side. I hope you know that!" she said, smacking her lips.

"I do, but I got more than just that lil shit for you, just wait." He promised, knowing what he had in store for her. "I gotta go though, send me a picture of your hair when it's finished."

"I'll think about it." She huffed, hanging up the phone in his ear. D'Mani chuckled to himself at how hard she was trying to play it. He couldn't say that she was ready yet, but he knew by the end of the night her ass was gone be right back with him.

Hours later, Mani stood outside of the Aria restaurant waiting on the town car that Anastasia was riding in to pull up. He had gotten shaped up earlier in the day once he'd finished all of his running and had still made it home in time to get dressed before Stasia arrived. He knew he was looking good in the black Dolce & Gabbana suit he'd picked out. Alyssa had assured him that Stasia was on her way not too long ago and the staff had just finished putting the final touches on the restaurant since he'd had it shut down for the night. D'Mani adjusted his silk tie as the sleek town car stopped right in front of him. He didn't wait for the driver to get out as he made his way to the curb and hurried to open the door for her himself. As soon as she placed her thick legs out of the car and stood in front of him, D'Mani bit his lips and then let a slow smile grace his face. Stasia looked good enough to eat literally, and he had to stop himself from saying *fuck dinner* and going straight to a hotel.

"Damn, you look good as fuck right now baby!" he said, pulling her into a hug and planting a light kiss on her neck. He didn't miss the moan she let slip out.

"Thanks, you don't look so bad yourself." She smirked and smoothed a hand over his lapel once they'd pulled apart. D'Mani took her hand in his and led her into the dimly lit restaurant, where the staff stood in a line to greet them. She looked around before turning to him in surprise. "You shut the restaurant down?"

"Hell yeah, I want you all to myself." She let out a small giggle and her cheeks flushed red.

"Pullin' out the big guns huh?" she questioned, not even knowing that it was light work compared to what he had in store for her.

"Only the best for you ma."

"Mmmhmm," she gave him a look before walking ahead a few steps and being greeted by each of the eight staff members. "So which one of these tables would you like for me to sit down at?" D'Mani followed behind her with his hands folded in front of him, hypnotized by the sway of her thick hips.

"None of them," he said, stopping her in her tracks. Confusion covered her face as he reached her. "We're goin' downstairs."

"Downstairs?"

"Yeah man downstairs, look, you trust me right?"

"Yeah... about as far as I can throw yo big ass." D'Mani narrowed his eyes at her smart comment, but chose not to let it ruin their night, especially since he was the reason she felt that way.

"Mannnnn, bring yo ass on." He grumbled as they were led to the wine cellar downstairs where their table awaited. Once they were seated, the chef and owner Gerry came out to greet them. Him and D'Mani had met earlier that day and the fact that Mani had covered whatever the chef might lose by closing the place down for him, he was anxious to get the couple whatever they wanted. He was going to make them his take on the classic filet mignon with a twist. They ordered the best bottle of wine the restaurant offered there, and after a few glasses, Anastasia loosened up. By the time they finished their dinner, she had moved closer to him in the booth and touching him lightly. She was feeling herself; he could tell by how giggly she was, but he wasn't complaining.

"Stasia, I wanted to run somethin' by you right quick." D'Mani said, holding her hand in his after she took her last bite of dessert.

"Umm... okay." Her voice came out uneasy like she wasn't sure what he was going to spring on her.

"It seem like ever since we met, it's been shit that we had to overcome together and even though it ain't been easy, *we* always got through what we needed to. I know that's because *we* belong with each other. I know I fucked shit up with us recently, but if you give me a chance to make it right, I will." He said sincerely and reached into his pocket to pull out the six-carat princess cut diamond ring that he had bought for her. "I'll spend the rest of my life making it right. I love you, will you do me the honor of being mine forever?"

Anastasia had tears brimming her eyes as she looked from D'Mani to the beautiful ring in his hand. "I don't want you to feel like this is what you have to do for my forgiveness D'Mani." She told him with a small shake of her head.

"Naw I want you to accept *because* you forgive me. I can deal with a lot of shit, but I been miserable as fuck without you baby for real. I need you, and I ain't tryna let yo ass go, so you bouta take a nigga's ring and make me honest?"

"Awwww yes! Yes I'll marry you!" she shrieked, allowing him to slide the ring on her finger. D'Mani released a sigh of relief, thankful that she was willing to be his wife and give him a second chance. She kissed him as she squealed happily. He knew that they had some more issues to work out, but the main one was taken care of and he was happy that there was one less thing on his to do list.

16

Soft cries coming from Alana caused Corey and Alyssa to slowly awaken. Tossing the covers back, Alyssa got out of bed to tend to the baby. Instead of going back to sleep, he sat up in bed and watched his wife as she fed their daughter. They had only been home for a day and Corey was enjoying every moment of it, but what he loved the most was lying next to his wife again. Being able to be with her full time again was all he really wanted and thanks to their daughter, Corey was able to do that.

As he continued to stare at his wife in admiration, Alyssa's eyes shifted in his direction. Locking eyes with each other, Corey couldn't help but smile.

"What you over there smiling for?"

"How beautiful you look holding our child," he admitted.

"Aww. Thanks bae," she beamed.

Corey climbed out of bed, walked over to the rocking chair she was sitting in, and kissed her forehead. Heading into the bathroom, the ringing of Alyssa's cell phone stopped him in his tracks. Corey snatched the phone off the nightstand and when he saw that it was the rehab calling, he handed the phone to her to answer it, but she silenced the call.

"The damn rehab has been blowing my phone up ever since I was in the hospital. They've left me like five voice-mails," she shook her head. "What did they say when you told them you I was giving birth?"

"I didn't tell them *shit*. When Stasia called me, I told my homie what the deal was and he drove me to the hospital."

"You broke out of rehab Corey?"

"How else was I supposed to get to you Lyssa?"

"You coulda at least told them that you were leaving and when you would be back," she huffed.

"Be back? Do you hear yourself right now? You really think I'm gonna leave you and my child here while I go back to finish my time at the rehab?" Corey glared at her. "You think me being there is more important than me being here with my family?"

"I didn't say that Corey."

"Then what the fuck are you saying Alyssa?" He raised his voice which caused the baby to cry a little.

"You know I want you here with us, but I also want you to be fully recovered. You've been doing good and I don't want you to relapse," she answered sincerely.

"Bae, I've been around alcohol and drugs on more than one occasion and haven't been tempted to try anything. I'm good, Alyssa," he assured her. "So, when they call you back, just let them know that I won't be coming back. Aight?"

"Okay baby," she gave him a small smile.

Pecking her lips, Corey strolled into the bathroom to freshen up. As he brushed his teeth, Corey couldn't help but to feel as though his wife didn't want him around, but instead of letting it get the best of him, he dismissed his ill feelings and finished up in the bathroom. Drying his face with the towel, he walked back into the bedroom where he saw Alyssa and the baby sleeping. Removing the baby from her hands and placing her inside the basinet, Corey walked out the room and down to the basement where he saw his brothers smoking. He gave them all handshakes before sitting in one of the nearby chairs.

"The fuck y'all down here talking about?" Corey asked.

"The same shit we always talking about Pinky," Mani chuckled and the others followed suit.

"But for real though. We weren't talking about shit that you don't know already bro. Money is still flowing and our enemies are still at large," Mari chimed in.

"Speaking of enemies, I got a problem I need help solving," Corey spoke up.

"Wassup?" J.R. finished the rest of the blunt.

"The niggas that almost killed me a few months, I found out that he's the brother of the nigga I killed. I got word that he got flunkies looking for me and shit and I need to find him before he finds me."

"Do you know where he be at?" Mani questioned.

"He spends most of his time in North Atlanta at a warehouse he turned into a gambling spot. Lou used to run it, but his brother Blue took over. One of the chicks that works at the rehab has been keeping tabs on him for me, but now that I'm home, I can keep tabs on the nigga myself."

"And how'd you find this out?" Mani leaned forward on the couch.

"One of the niggas in rehab told me."

They all gave him a sideways look.

"I know what y'all are thinking, but he's not one of the motherfuckas that's whacked outta his mind. Larry informed me that me and him got a few enemies in common, but Blue was the only one he told me about. Dude seems cool but I'm still trying to figure him out. Some shit happened in there that I was trying to get to the bottom of, but Alyssa had the baby. That's the *only* reason why I wanted to stay in there," Corey confessed.

Mani nodded his head in understanding. The room fell silent for a minute, each in their own thoughts. By the expressions on their faces, Corey felt like they were going to tell him that he was on his own but he knew better than that.

"When do you wanna move out? Mari spoke.

"Shit! The sooner the better. As soon as we get this shit out the way, we can put all our focus on Tessa."

"As soon as you're up to it, the first thing you do is to make sure Blue's locations check out. That chick that was working for you coulda been lying. As far as the nigga that gave you the info, keep close tabs on him. That nigga might be useful or we might have to put a bullet through him," Mani instructed.

"No problem."

Wrapping up their conversation, they exited the basement and went their separate ways. As he headed back to his room, a text came through on his phone. Corey pulled his phone out of his sweatpants pocket and saw that it was from Deana.

Deana: You coulda told me what was going on with you Corey. I've been looking for you for the past few days and I just found out that you're not coming back to the rehab. Smh. Just text me if you need me. You know I'm always here for you

Corey shook his head at the message as he placed the phone back in his pocket. He didn't have any intentions on reaching out to Deana again because he no longer needed her services. Whatever feelings she had for him was not his problem because she knew what it was from the door. Entering his room, Corey checked on his baby girl and when he saw that Alana was still sleep, he got into bed and cuddled up with his wife.

✣ 17 ✣

"It's no problem… I'll make it work," Mari heard Drea say as he entered into the bedroom.

Once she looked up and saw him, she ended the call without even saying goodbye to whoever was on the other end. That was the *third* time that Mari had caught her whispering on the phone and hanging up when he walked in. He had let the shit slide long enough. He had been trying to keep the peace, but he had had enough.

"Drea, what's up wit all the whispering and shit and you hangi…"

Before Mari could get the rest of his question out of his mouth, Drea was on her knees in front of him with his dick in her mouth. It had been so long that they had been intimate, all of the thoughts that Mari once had were instantly replaced with pleasure. His dick was rock hard in no time. He moaned and grabbed Drea's head and kept it in place. The shit felt good as fuck as she teased, slurped, licked, and sucked his dick and balls. Mari tried to fuck her mouth, but she let him know that she was the one in charge. Drea aggressively pushed him to the bed and pulled his pants the rest of the way down and got back to work without missing a beat. With the moans that she was making, Mari didn't know who was enjoying it the most, but he was in heaven.

"Shit... got damn baby," Mari grunted.

"You like that?" she looked up and purred.

"Hell fuckin' yeah! Don't stop!"

Drea granted his wish and just when he thought it couldn't get any better, she turned it up a notch and made his toes curl. When Mari felt himself about to cum, he could tell that Drea knew because she stood up, lifted her skirt up, and then eased down to onto his dick.

"Wait... you good?" he asked.

"Better than good," she replied as she kissed him and began riding his dick.

It had been a few weeks since Drea suffered the miscarriage that resulted from the shooting and that meant Mari hadn't had any pussy since then because she was pissed off at him. To say that he was feeling good at that moment would have been an understatement. The way that Drea's pussy curved to his dick had him ready to bust. With the way that she was putting it on him, Mari wasn't going to be able to hold out much longer; and if he didn't know any better, he swore that those were her exact intentions. It had been a long ass time since she had taken control the way that she was doing, but he was just glad to be getting some instead of beating his meat. Drea's legs began to shake uncontrollably as she rode him. When Mari heard her sex cries get louder, it sent him over the edge. They both came and Mari knew that he had some shit to handle, but he wanted to cuddle a little bit.

Mari felt Drea's weight shift and when he reached to pull her down, she jerked away. The shit threw him for a loop, and before he could address the shit, she slammed and locked the bathroom door.

"Yo Drea... what the fuck?" he got up and knocked.

"I just needed some D'Mari. I'm still pissed at your ass, but the dick was good," she snapped.

"What the fuck?" he fumed.

Drea had him fucked up, treating him like he was some jump off. Mari stared at the bathroom door and thought about how she really had just pulled some straight nigga shit. He almost knocked on the door but decided against it when he heard the shower come on. The thought of his wife being with another man had Mari seeing red. Just when things should have been getting better for the Mitchell's, they appeared to be drifting farther apart. Mari went and grabbed an all-black outfit, his black polo boots, and a few other things and made his way to the bathroom that was in the hall.

After showering and getting dressed, he went to the basement, being sure to dodge all of the women, especially his mother, mother in-law, and Aunt Shirley. It was time to get down to business. When he made it to the basement, J.R. was already sitting at the table with a half full bottle of Remy. Mari wasted no time grabbing the bottle and turning it up. It was almost seven o'clock which meant that it was almost show time.

"How long you been down here? This bottle was new, wasn't it?" Mari asked after he sat the Remy bottle back down.

"Hell yeah... gotta drink to stay sane round this mu'fucka," J.R. took another swig.

"Tell me about it," Mari thought about his new problem.

"These damn Holiday sisters... it's either hot or cold wit em," Mari continued.

"Right, but they'll be alright. We gotta stay focused and handle this shit so we can get back to our lives. The longer these damn sisters live together, the more they team up against our asses," J.R. expressed.

"It'll all be over soon. Your girl ready?" Mari quizzed.

Before J.R. could answer, his phone buzzed. He read a text, down the rest of the liquor, and then stood up.

"Let's go get this muthafucka!" he announced and that was music to D'Mari's ears.

18

Shit had been crazy the last couple of days. Every time J.R. took two steps forward, he felt like he was being pulled five steps back. His relationship with Lexi was being tested like never before. After telling her the truth about Kellz, she still didn't believe him. He partially understood because the story did sound like some bullshit; but since he had never given her a reason not to trust him before, she should just chill. J.R. had been spending most of his time either in the streets or in the basement with the rest of the guys. Sometimes, they would just sit in the car and talk, just to be away from the Holiday sisters.

J.R. downed the last of the Remy he was drinking and headed upstairs to get his phone off the charger, so him and D'Mari could bounce. He quickly slipped through the house trying to avoid any unnecessary stares but was caught in the hallway by Aunt Shirley.

"What up?" J.R. nodded his head, passing her and heading towards the room.

"Don't *what up* me, witcho cheating ass," she replied, rolling her eyes.

"Man, what you talking about now?" he asked, growing more aggravated by the minute.

"Hmph, I ain't the one to gossip so you ain't heard this from me BUT.... Me and Lexi been in there for the past 30 minutes trying to unlock yo phone," she replied.

"You know she told me about the little bitch you got pregnant at the hotel," she continued.

"Bitch? Pregnant? What the fuck......"

Instead of continuing the conversation with Aunt Shirley, J.R. stormed off towards the bedroom where he found Lexi getting dressed. When he entered the room, she looked at him, rolled her eyes, and finished up. J.R. went to his phone, which was still plugged up on the nightstand and picked it up. Seeing that his phone was disabled from too many attempts with the wrong password, pissed him off even more.

"Why the fuck you going through my shit?" he turned around and asked.

"Why the fuck yo shit got a lock on it? ALL OF A SUDDEN?!" she snapped.

"Cuz I pay that bill." He simply advised her.

"I just find it funny how you ain't never had a lock on yo shit before, but when you get caught up, now there's a lock on your phone."

"Caught up? Who the fuck got caught up? I explained to you *exactly* what happened."

"And it still sound like *some bullshit* to me," Lexi replied.

"I ain't got time for this shit." He said under his breath before snatching up his keys and walking out the door.

He made it to the bottom of the stairs and called out for D'Mari who was actually walking up from behind him.

"Nigga you straight?" he quizzed, noticing the look on his homie's face.

"This goofy ass bitc----" J.R. paused when he noticed

Lyssa, Stasia, and Drea sitting at the kitchen table, waiting on him to get *disrespectful* so they could snap.

"Let's go bro." D'Mari laughed, noticing the stares and heavy tension in the room.

The duo did as they said and left out the house, heading to a motel right off Peachtree Road. The entire ride consisted of them smoking and trying to clear their mind. J.R. knew Mari was dealing with shit with his wife, just like the rest of the men in the house. He couldn't wait until it was all over so things could go back to normal. Lexi was due in a month and half and that was his deadline to have everything handled. There was no way his son or daughter was going to be born with a target on its head. He would die before he allowed that to happen.

"Now, you sure this gon' work?" Mari asked as they pulled into the parking lot.

"I been planning this shit for over a week now, it better work," he replied, tossing the small blunt out the window.

"Aight, I'm with you. Let's do this."

Mari checked his gun while J.R. did the same thing. He hoped and prayed that shit actually ran as smooth in real life as it did in his head. He knew one wrong move, and everyone involved would be dead.

"I bet that's the nigga car right there," Mari said, pointing to a midnight blue Maserati.

"Bitch ass nigga drives a Maserati but take his bitches to this raggedy ass motel to fuck," he shrugged, zipping his black hoodie all the way up.

"What room you say again?" Mari quizzed, walking on the side of J.R.

"Room 305." He recalled from the text message sent to him earlier.

"Bet, let's go handle this shit." Mari stated, pulling both guns out, leading the way.

They took the stairs to the third floor of the motel. When they arrived at the room, they stood by the door and listened.

"It should be open," J.R. whispered.

Mari used that as an invitation to burst in, but the door swung open before he could.

Gripping the trigger and ready to shoot whoever was on the other end, J.R. nerves relaxed a little when noticed it was Kellz.

"What the fuck you doing out here and you supposed to be in there handling....."

J.R. paused when Kellz stepped to the side. It wasn't until then he noticed a bloody body on the bed. J.R. pushed her back in the room; Mari followed behind him and closed the door.

"I got tired of waiting on y'all," she smiled, bending down and grabbing her shoes.

Both men looked on in awe. Kellz already turned J.R. on but now, he was attracted to her on whole another level.

"Let me wash this filth off of me. I'll be back," she stated, disappearing out of the small room.

"That bitch bad!" Mari spoke as soon as the bathroom door closed.

"Nigga, now you see why she got me ready to *risk it all*," J.R. laughed, looking at the work Kellz had just put in.

"You say she's Julian home girl, right?" Mari questioned.

"Yup!"

Just as J.R. was about to continue, Kellz joined them back in the room.

"I'm just curious, how you pull this off so fast?" Mari asked her.

"Niggas love a big butt and smile," she giggled before continuing.

"But I did everything J.R. told me to do," she glanced at him and winked.

"I found out where the nigga kicked it at. Once I told him I was sixteen, he was ready to go," she explained.

"Sick bastard," Mari grimaced, shaking his head.

"Y'all have no idea," Kellz chimed in, shaking her head as well.

When Jessica said she would help bring down Tessa's cartel, she meant that. The first brother on their shit list was Elliot. He was the oldest of the clan and the sickest. Jessica explained how he had a fetish for young girls. He liked them thick, young, and beautiful. Jessica told stories about how he would pry on these young girls, sitting outside of random high schools and luring them in with his money. All that power and pussy, his weakness is what got him killed.

"You sure y'all wasn't followed?" J.R. pulled the curtain back a smidge and asked.

"Positive. The nigga was so thirsty," Kellz assured him.

"But damn, did you have to cut off the man's dick?" Mari asked as he stood over Elliot's dead body.

"Yeah I did," she giggled, looking over her work.

J.R. walked from the window and over to the body to get a closer look. Not only had she cut off his dick, she put a bullet hole the size of a crater in his chest. Impressed, he turned to her and thanked her. The original plan was to catch him with this pants down and murk him that way, but Kellz did her own thang, which was fine by him. He planned on repaying her tremendously since she had made shit so much easier for him.

"Aight, looks like we done here," Mari stated, pulling out his phone.

J.R. knew he was calling the cleanup crew, but he stopped him.

"Leave that nigga here so his people can find him."

Mari looked up and smiled, “Oh we sending messages now huh?” he smirked.

“They started it with my sister’s finger,” he barked.

“Let’s go then,” Kellz stated, heading towards the door.

“One down, two more to go,” J.R. canted as he made his way out of the motel room.

19

"Wait, come again now?"

D'Mani let out a heavy sigh not really wanting to repeat what he'd just told Anastasia but knowing that he would have to. It had been a couple days since the proposal and so far, everything had been good. Stasia seemed happier than ever and had started sleeping in the same room as him again. The sisters weren't all giving him the silent treatment and he was able to spend time with Kyler freely. Now seemed like a terrible ass time to drop the bomb on everyone that he would have to move Cheyanne into the house with them. Stasia was already looking pissed, so he could just imagine how her highly hormonal sisters were going to react.

"Anastasia the girl on her deathbed, and..."

"So! You can't hire some damn body to work with her at HER HOUSE!?" she fumed, pacing their room. D'Mani understood how uncomfortable the living arrangements would be for her, but at the same time, Cheyanne was the mother of his child and he just wouldn't feel right letting her be alone for her final days.

"I can't do that," D'Mani shook his head. "Imani wouldn't be able to stay there and regardless of her health, I know she gone wanna have access to baby girl every day."

"Naw it seem like she want access to yo ass every day!" she stopped her constant back and forth and looked at him through squinted eyes. "Nigga, is this the reason you proposed? Huh? You think a ring was gone placate me while you moved this bitch in here?!" she went to slap him, but D'Mani blocked it and grabbed both of her wrists.

"Yo, chill the fuck out Stasia! You trippin' man. I gave yo ass that ring because I love you and I wanna be with you, it ain't have *shit* to do with Cheyanne! I don't want her at all, that shit was a mistake, there ain't no feelings there... but at the same time, she's my baby's mother and I can't allow her to die alone! Would you even wanna be with a nigga that would do some shit like that?" she'd stopped struggling to get out of his grasp and he could see that she was letting the question sink in. Finally, she snatched away, letting out a deep sigh.

"No, I wouldn't, but I also still don't trust that bitch, D'Mani. She's not as innocent as she's lettin' on and I hope that yo monkey ass sees it before it's too late."

With that said, she left, making sure to slam the door behind her. D'Mani sat back down on the bed and put his head in his hands. He had known that telling Anastasia about moving Cheyanne in wasn't going to be easy, and he thought he was prepared. The last thing that he wanted was to make her feel like his intentions weren't honorable, but it was clear that it was Cheyanne that she was leery of. For some reason, her words bothered him, but Cheyanne hadn't given him a reason to be suspicious of her the whole time that she'd come back into their lives. He shook off his thoughts and got dressed for the day in some jeans, a plain Nike t-shirt, and his space jam Jordan's.

When he made it downstairs, Mani felt the tension as

each of the sisters and Aunt Shirley sat eyeballing him evilly. He looked at Stasia who was sitting on the couch next to Lexi, holding a wine glass to her lips, wondering where his brother and everybody else was. D'Mani started to back out of the room, but he didn't. He was just trying to be nice and they were all acting like he had asked Stasia to be polygamous or some shit. Instead, he rolled his eyes in annoyance, causing Lexi to gasp in shock.

"You know you got some fuckin' nerve nigga!" she scoffed.

"Calm down boo, you can't be getting worked up and stressin' that baby, let me handle it." Aunt Shirley said before turning to D'Mani with a frown. "Nigga you got some fuckin' nerve! How you tryna out pimp me boy!"

"Really Aunty Shirley?" Anastasia asked, looking mortified by her Aunt, even though everyone knew that she was crazy as hell.

"Nah Aunty not right now," Lexi told her, putting her hand over her face as if to hide .

"What? I can't be honest? Y'all lil heffas gone learn that y'all don't control my mouth! I say whatever the hell I want to and that nigga a pimp!" Shirley huffed.

"Listen, like I told Stasia, this move is *only* because she wants to spend her last days with her daughter, and I'm not risking her being alone with Imani again. I'm not tryna be funny, sneaky, a pimp, or any of the other shit y'all cookin' up in them twisted minds of yours." D'Mani told them all, making sure that he looked each one in the eye. The sisters all looked at Anastasia like they were going to follow her lead on it while Shirley twisted her lips at him in disbelief.

"Okay, but as soon as I see some bullshit, she getting her sick ass beat!" Stasia spat and stormed out of the room with her sisters all trailing behind her, giving him the stank face. Shirley stayed behind and walked up to him.

"I joke a whole lot, but I'm tellin' you now... if one swing, we all swing lil nigga!" she said in a low voice before punching one fist into the other. "You better make sure yo lil hoe knows that!" She threw over her shoulder as she disappeared down the same hall as her nieces.

D'Mani shook his head and pulled his phone out to call his brother as he hurried out of the front door. D'Mari picked up on the third ring.

"Wassup you, ain't dead yet?" he laughed into the receiver as soon as he answered.

"Nigga that shit ain't funny! Where the fuck all y'all niggas at? Left me in there by myself and shit!" D'Mani huffed, irritated by the howl of laughter his brother let out at his plight.

"What the fuck? You thought we was bouta catch that heat cause you wanna move yo baby mama in, *the one* that you *cheated* with?! You got me fucked up bro... me and Drea got our own shit goin' on! You ain't bouta get me mixed up in that!"

D'Mani pulled the phone away from his ear as he got into the driver's seat and made sure that it was his brother he was talking to because there was no way his brother was gone leave him hanging like that.

"Mannn... yo scary ass!"

"Aye call me what you want, but you ain't gone call me *pussyless*!" D'Mari laughed in his ear. Not wanting to hear him crack anymore jokes, D'Mani hung up the phone and pulled out of the driveway, headed to the hospital. He couldn't believe that nigga was gone leave him out to dry like that. It wasn't even no point in calling Corey and J.R. cause they more than likely had the same stance on the situation. What everybody failed to realize though was that he wasn't trying to hurt Stasia at all. He only wanted the woman's last days to be spent with his daughter. If there was another way that he could make that happen without putting Imani at risk, he would have sought it out, but that was the best solution for him.

The look on Anastasia's face was still on his mind when he made it to the hospital, and he hoped that Cheyanne didn't pick up on his vibe when he walked in because he wasn't trying to stress her out. The move was going to be news to her too, and he was sure that she was not going to like it.

When he made it up to her room, Mani was surprised to see that Cheyanne was already dressed and ready to go, even though they hadn't set a specific time for her discharge. She smiled weakly as soon as she saw him and he forced one back. It was hard to tell that she was the same woman who had just come into his life with his daughter not too long ago. She looked pale and weak. Even her hair looked dull with little to no life. There were bags under her eyes and her lips looked cracked despite how shiny they were. He tried to hide the pity that he was sure showed on his face.

"Hey beautiful." He bent to give her a kiss on the cheek, careful not to hurt her.

"Ha, you got jokes huh?" she chuckled bitterly. "Ain't nothin' beautiful about what you seeing." She rolled her eyes and it made her look dead.

"I'm not goin' back and forth with you, I said what I said," he told her, taking a seat on her made up bed.

"Well, if you insist... where's Imani?" she turned her wheelchair so that she could face him.

"She's at home. I figured that it would be easier to get you out of here without her lil butt getting in the way." She nodded solemnly and he could tell that it saddened her, but he wasn't trying to have to keep up with Imani and move her mother. He had never known how hard it was to do anything productive with a little kid around until Imani came into the picture.

"True." She agreed just as a nurse entered the room.

"Hello, you must be here to take Cheyanne home," she greeted me with her hand out. "I'm Danielle."

"D'Mani," he said, giving her one shake before releasing her cold ass hand. She giggled at nothing and began giving them both her discharge instructions while constantly giving him a flirtatious look. D'Mani was used to the female attention, but he felt like right then was just downright inappropriate. He ignored the looks and focused on her care instructions even though he planned on hiring someone to care for her.

"Welp, that's it. It was a pleasure working with you honey," she told Cheyanne before turning to D'Mani. "And if you need someone for homecare, I'm definitely available."

"Nah I already got a healthcare aide, thanks tho." He sneered and snatched the papers out of her hand. A shocked look crossed her face before she left out of the room, leaving Cheyanne chuckling.

"You still mean as hell."

"Bitch shouldn't have been tryna flirt." He told her with a frown. Cheyanne just shook her head as he gathered the rest of her things which was just a duffle bag and a plastic bag that the hospital was sending her with.

Once he got them downstairs, he loaded up the truck and helped her into the backseat before he climbed in himself. He still hadn't figured out how he was going to break the news to her that she was going to be moving into the house with him and Stasia. D'Mani cut the radio all the way up so that he could try and figure something out, but by the time he pulled into the driveway at the house, he still hadn't come up with anything.

"Are we pickin' up Imani?" Cheyanne asked in confusion. D'Mani cut the radio down and turned in his seat so that he could tell her what he'd been dreading, but he figured if he got through telling the Holiday sisters then Cheyanne would be a piece of cake.

"Ummmm, no... this is where I'm taking you." D'Mani told her.

"But this ain't my damn house!" she looked between him and the house clearly irritated. "Whose house is this?"

"Our house for the time being," he said slowly. Cheyanne narrowed her eyes.

"What you mean *our*, D'Mani? Who lives here?"

"Me......Imani......Stasia... her sisters and their niggas." Her eyes widened and her breathing picked up, letting him know that she was about to start panicking.

"You mean to tell me that you want *me* to live in a house with *a woman* whose man *I slept with* and *her sisters?!*"

"Listen... I already told them about you comin' here. They may not be happy, but ain't nobody gone bother you." He promised while she shook her head and mumbled under her breathe. "Trust me... it will be okay."

"How you know? Have you *ever* lived under the same roof as *somebody* who *slept* with *your woman* before?" she shrieked.

"Nah, but you're not in a position to be alone, especially with Imani. Now I already told you that everybody knows you coming. I ain't gone let nothing happen to you." He spoke firmly and it took a minute, but she finally nodded like she understood and was ready to go inside.

D'Mani took her bags inside first and placed them near the door before going back out to get her. When he first went in, the house was dead silent like no one was there, but as soon as he helped Cheyanne inside, they were stopped in their tracks by the sight of the Holiday sisters and Aunt Shirley all lined up like they were about to tag team the girl. Cheyanne drew in a breath and dropped her head as D'Mani helped her past the ladies who all had on their war faces and were mumbling shit under their breaths. Thankfully, none of them made an attempt, but it was clear that they were trying to intimidate the girl. Even Drea was out there and he expected her to be the most mature of them all. One thing was for certain and two things were for sure, they were not going to make this easy on him or Cheyanne. D'Mani just prayed that nobody got hurt, and when he said nobody, he meant Cheyanne.

20

Corey sat on the edge tying up his Nike boots while Young Jeezy's *'Hustlaz Ambition'* played on his phone. He'd been keeping tabs on Blue for over a week and the time had come to lay that nigga and his squad to rest. Corey knew every move he made like the back of his hand and when he discovered where that nigga rested his head at, his ass felt like he struck gold. Thinking about how Blue and his squad ran up in the house that he shared with his wife and came out with a duffle bag full of money and jewelry had him seeing red. They fucked his house up from top to bottom, making sure they left their mark on the living room wall. Relieved that they didn't hit all of his stash spots, Corey took the few thousands back to the mansion and locked up the house like nothing happened. On a daily, Blue would have one of his flunkies drive around to the trap houses Corey used to visit just to see if he was there. He knew Blue was tired of coming up empty handed but his search for Corey would soon be coming to an end.

Throwing on his black hoodie and tucking his ski mask in his pocket, Corey killed the music on his phone as Alyssa came walking through their bedroom door with their daughter in her arms. She walked past him like he wasn't even there and placed Alana in her basinet. Shaking his head, Corey snatched up his keys and was about to head out the door until Alyssa threw a pillow at his back.

"What'd you do that for, Alyssa?" he turned around to face her.

"So, you just gonna walk outta here without saying anything?" she stood in the middle of the floor with her arms folded over her chest.

"Kill the bullshit, man. You've been acting like a nigga don't even exist since we got home from the hospital. I told you I wasn't going back to the rehab, so I can be here for you and baby girl, but you act like you don't want me here. I decided to let that shit ride and move forward and the next thing I know, you got this icy ass demeanor and ain't got no rap for me. I ask you what's wrong, you don't respond. I'm not gonna force you to talk Lyssa and I'm not gonna keep kissing ya ass either. So whenever ya ass is ready to be an adult, holla at me," he stated harshly.

"Nah. How about you go holla at ya other bitch instead?" Alyssa shouted.

"What the fuck are you talking about?"

"Oh, so now you playing dumb huh?"

"Look man, I gotta go. I'll deal with you when I get back, aight? Cuz you bugging."

"Fuck you, Corey!" she yelled as he walked out the door.

Jogging down the stairs, Corey darted out the house and hopped in the passenger's side of the black Yukon Denali with his brothers.

"What the fuck took you so long?" J.R. questioned.

"Alyssa held me up," Corey let out a sigh of frustration.

"Say less," Mari chuckled. "Where are we going?"

"College Park. They stay at this trap house until midnight. So, they ain't moving no time soon."

"Cool. Let's ride," Mani spoke from the back seat.

As they headed towards their destination, Corey filled them in on how many people could be in the house and what went down in there. Thursday nights were the day they counted up the money and invited bitches over to party. After he finished giving his brothers the details, Corey thought back to when those niggas almost took his life and that shit was enough to get his fucking adrenaline going. Forty minutes later, J.R turned onto a run-down block where most of the houses were abandoned. Killing the lights on the truck, he parked the Yukon a few feet away from the house before grabbing their guns and jumping out the truck with Corey leading the pack. As they piled on the front porch, he gave them a signal before kicking in the front door with their guns blazing. Shot after shot rang out as bodies instantly hit the floor. Niggas came from upstairs and the basement and The Rock Boyz laid they asses down in a heartbeat. Admiring the mess of bloody bodies, Corey ran downstairs to the basement where a mess of fifties and hundreds were scattered all over the tables and floor. Snatching up a duffle bag, he filled it up until the bag was too full to zip.

On his way up the stairs, he heard movement coming from behind a door that was down there with a pad lock on it. Noticing the lock wasn't there, Corey aimed his gun at the door before swinging it open and moving to the side just in time to miss the barrage of bullets that was flying out. When the shooting stopped, a man stepped out and Corey hit him in the head with the butt of his gun, causing him to drop to the floor screaming out in pain. When Corey's eyes recognized the nigga that was cowering out in pain, a smirk appeared on his face as he aimed his gun at Blue's dome.

Locking eyes with the man that was about to take his life, Blue let out a chuckle.

"I'll see you in hell motherfucka."

Corey pulled the trigger, sending a bullet through his head, ending his life instantly. As Blue's blood decorated the concrete floor, Corey grabbed the duffle bag full of money and ran upstairs and out the door where his brothers were waiting for him in the truck. Feeling like the weight was lifted off his shoulders, Corey was content with the fact that his enemies were no longer a problem and they could focus on their major issues. Feeling his phone vibrate in his pocket, Corey let out an irritated sigh when he saw Deana texting him. When he saw that she sent him a long paragraph to read, he was about to put his phone back in his pocket until he saw the last time she had texted him was two days before. Scrolling up to the last message he read from her, which was over a week ago, Corey saw that she had sent him a total of six messages that he never saw. Replaying the conversation he had with Alyssa before he left, he laid his head back as shit became clear to him. Alyssa went through his phone and read his messages from Deana. Feeling fucked up, Corey was going to have to do the very thing he said he wouldn't do, which was kiss her ass.

21

It had been a few days since Drea fucked him like a nigga, and as the days passed, it didn't get any better. She did talk to him, but the shit was on her terms and Mari needed to find out what the fuck she had going on. He knew Drea held onto shit, but normally it didn't last that long. He wondered if he had truly driven her away with his actions. Mari had left the spot after handling a little business and pulled up at their home away from home at ten minutes after two. It was supposed to be a laid back Saturday, but duty called and he had to answer. The rest of the guys were chillin' in the basement and Mari couldn't wait to join them. He had overheard Lexi and Drea talking about shopping and knew that they were still out. All of the sisters normally did shit together, but since Alyssa had her baby, they was doing shit in pairs and giving each other breaks.

Mari walked into the house and the first person that he saw was Cheyanne. She looked scared as hell, and he really couldn't help but to chuckle at the fact that his brother had managed to have *two* women living under the same roof. Cheyanne was barely out of her room, so he knew just by seeing her, the other two sisters must have been in one of their rooms or they may have left also.

"Hi Cheyanne," he spoke before she was completely out of dodge.

"Hi," she replied and then went about her way.

Mari shook his head and went to the twin's room. He hated that the poor girl was dying. Surprisingly, the Holiday sisters had left her alone and he really hoped that his brother could have a serious conversation with Stasia and Cheyanne before the girl took her last breath. They were dealing with some serious shit since a kid was involved and even though Mari didn't know shit about Cheyanne, he felt that she deserved to know the woman who would take care of her daughter that she was leaving behind . Both of his kids were sleeping peacefully, so he didn't wake them up; he simply kissed both of them and exited the room. Mari was headed to his room to change his clothes, but he said *fuck it*, made a detour, and went straight to the basement.

As soon as he opened the door, the music was blasting and Mari could tell that the drinks were already flowing. Mani and J.R. were talking shit while playing NBA2K. Corey was sitting there texting someone, but he looked up and spoke when Mari entered. Without wasting any time at all, Mari grabbed the Remy off the table and poured himself a double shot.

"Nigga stop cheating," J.R. knocked Mani's controller out of his hand.

"Nigga ain't nobody cheating. Take this ass whoopin' like a man," Mani laughed.

"Fuck you... rack 'em up Mari. I'm sick of yo cheating ass brother," J.R. said as he walked towards the table and grabbed some liquor.

"I'm up," Corey said and took J.R.'s spot.

Mari and J.R. went and started a game of pool. Halfway

through the game, Mari's phone vibrated and he pulled it out, seeing a text from *that* bitch that he couldn't get rid of. He had been ignoring her ass, but the message that he read pissed him the fuck off. It also let him know that he needed to get a handle on her psycho ass before she ruined his life.

"Fuck wrong wit you nigga?" J.R. quizzed.

"I'm sick of this Janice bitch I was telling you about. She buggin' the fuck out," Mari vented.

"What the fuck she talmbout now?"

Mari simply handed J.R. his phone so that he could read the text.

"Maannn... go murk that bitch. What the fuck could she possibly have on you?"

"Ion know, but you finna go wit me to find out," Mari told him.

"Aww hell naw... I ain't getting in the middle of y'all bull-shit. Plus I gotta go and meet Kellz on some business in a minute."

"That makes it even better. I can have you and Kellz wit me so the shit don't look like no date or no shit like that. I'll have her meet us at the Taco Mac on Peachtree, so I can get this shit over wit," Mari explained.

"Y'all niggaz *always* getting me caught up in y'all shit," J.R. mumbled.

"Nigga you be getting *us* caught up in *yo* shit too so really we all in this shit together. Now come on so we can get this bullshit over wit," Mari headed towards the door.

"Yo we'll be back," Mari told Corey and Mani, but they were too busy talking shit to answer.

When he opened the door, Aunt Shirley almost fell inside and broke her neck.

"You tryna kill me nephew... damn!!" she fussed.

"What you doi... you know what? Never mind. Nah I'm

not tryna kill you. I just didn't know you was outside the door."

"Hit Em Up" by Tupac blasted through the speakers and Aunt Shirley started rapping like she was Tupac for real.

"We gotta go Auntie, but we'll be back," Mari told her and stepped around.

"Don't y'all go out there and be cheating on my sweet nieces. They ain't all that sweet, but I'm the *only* one who can say that shit."

Forty minutes later, Mari turned into the parking lot of Taco Mac and parked in the first spot that he saw. Being near the door wasn't important to him, he loved to park where there weren't too many cars to decrease the chances of his shit getting scratched. J.R. parked two spaces over from him about five minutes later. He didn't know why his boy just didn't ride with him at first, but when he saw Kellz in the passenger's seat, he figured the shit out. Mari got out and waited on J.R. and he heard him tell Kellz to hit the lock after she got off of the phone. They walked in and Mari asked for a booth near the back, but it was packed, so they ended up right in the middle. As soon as Mari and J.R. sat down, Kellz joined them. Mari couldn't help but to notice the stares that J.R. gave Kellz. He couldn't blame him; the girl was *bad* and he was glad that there was no harm in looking as long as you didn't touch.

"Hey guys... I haven't eaten here in forever, so I'm glad y'all picked this spot. What's goin' on?" Kellz spoke.

The waitress came over and took their orders and Janice walked in and sat down as soon as she left. The look that her and Kellz gave each other didn't go unnoticed. The two had to know each other and Mari got straight to the point.

"What the fuck is it that you want from me?"

"Damn baby... let's at least enjoy our meal first," Janice smirked.

"Clearly you don't know who the fuck I am... so let's try this once again. What the fuck do you want? I saw you one time at the facility while visiting my cousin and you acting like you know me. What the fuck is it that you want from me? And do you two know each other?" Mari seethed as he pointed at Kellz.

"Well, since you sick of my shit already... I figured *you* getting wit *me* would make you feel better since *your wife* is really friendly wit *my husband*," Janice said, catching D'Mari completely off guard.

"What the fuck you talking bout?" he asked, not showing any kinda emotions.

He had finally sent his PI a text to check into Janice and he couldn't wait until he got back in touch with him. The shit that she had just said really pissed him off, but he wouldn't dare let it show.

"Who yo husband?" J.R. chimed in.

"Let's let them handle that while we go handle our business babe," Kellz got up and reached for J.R.'s hand, but the look on his face and the voice that rang out let Mari know that the entire day was about to be shot to hell.

"IS *THIS* THE BITCH YOU WANT JEREMY??" Lexi screamed.

22

For as long as J.R. could remember, he had never broken a mirror, walked under a ladder, split a pole, or any other silly superstition belief that would have deemed him seven years of *bad luck*. The shit that he was currently going through was unbelievable and he knew he *must have* pissed off somebody higher up.

"Jeremy, *this* yo bitch huh?" Lexi snapped, walking closer to him and mushing him in the head.

"Look, it's not how it looks," Kellz stepped in, but Lexi quickly shot her down.

"Look bitch, speak when spoken to," Lexi yelled, causing everyone in the restaurant to look their way.

"I know y'all upset but....." Janice started to speak but was cut off by a fuming Drea.

"Did you NOT just hear that lecture on speaking when spoken to?" Andrea growled, causing Janice to close her mouth.

J.R. looked over at D'Mari who was just as shocked as he was. They could simply tell the truth to their women but even they knew that the story sounded crazy, but it was worth a shot.

"Lexi, this is Kellz, shorty from....."

"THE HOTEL?!" Lexi screamed, slipping out of her Guess jacket, ready to fight.

J.R. quickly stood to his feet. There she was, eight months pregnant, thinking she was about to attack someone. There was no way in hell he was going to allow them to come to blows.

"Imma just call me an Uber cuz this shit is too much for me," Kellz said, scooting her chair back and going around the table, the opposite way of Lexi.

"Bitch when I drop my load....." Lexi yelled out and Kellz stopped walking, cutting her off.

"You *still* ain't gon' do shit..." she replied, flipping Lexi the middle finger, disappearing out the door.

"Imma fuck that bitch uppppppppppp!" an angry Lexi yelled, trying her best to get to Kellz but J.R. held her back.

Finally calming down, she took a seat at the table as she caught her breath.

"Bitch you need to be catching a ride with your friend," Drea turned to Janice, who sat quietly at the table.

"Or you gon' be catching these hands," Lexi stood up quickly and shouted, taking a swing at Janice, catching her on the bridge of her nose.

Shocked, Janice stood up, ready to attack Lexi but was caught with a right hook from Drea. Drea's punch knocked Janice back in her seat while Lexi fought to grab her from the other side of the table.

"I'm sorry but I'm going to have to ask you guys to leave before we call the......"

The manager stopped talking in mid-sentence when he noticed the look on J.R's face.

"I'm so sorry but I'm going to have to ask you to leave

please," he repeated, this time avoiding eye contact with both of the guys.

J.R. and D'Mari somehow calmed the two sisters down. By the time they were done, Janice had dipped out and was nowhere to be found. Thankful for that, J.R tried to help Lexi place her coat back on so they could leave, but Lexi didn't allow him to touch her. Instead, she fought him away, cursing and screaming.

"I fuck'n' hate y—"

Lexi bent over in pain and grabbed her stomach, unable to complete her sentence.

"Baby, are you ok?" a concerned J.R. asked, placing his hand on the small of her back.

"I'm good, don't you fuck'n' touch m-"

Whatever pain Lexi was feeling cut her off again. This time, she grabbed onto the table to catch her balance.

"Fuck that! Come on, we going to the hospital," J.R. announced as he tried to rush her out of the door.

Drea ran over to Lexi's side and tried to figure out what was wrong as well. Neither of them had to wait for an answer because seconds later, Lexi's leggings were soak and wet.

"OH MY GOD! HER WATER BROKE!" Drea screamed out as the other customers excitedly looked on, some even pulling out their phones.

"Shit! Mari, help me get her in the car and y'all meet me at the hospital," J.R. ordered.

"Bullshit! I'm not riding with you. I'm getting in the car with Drea," Lexi replied.

"Alexis, right now ain't the time for your bullshit. You can be mad later but...."

"I'M NOT GETTING IN THE MUTHAFUCKER CAR WITH YOU! MEET US THERE!" she screamed at the top of her lungs.

Regardless of how much J.R. wanted to go back and forth

with her, he honestly didn't have the energy. Instead, he helped her inside of Drea's car and told Mari he'd follow him there and headed out.

Although Drea was a few cars ahead of him, J.R. still peeped how she dipped in and out of traffic. It still hadn't hit him yet that he was about to be a father. Lexi wasn't due for another three weeks, but the doctor let them know the last appointment that the baby was weighing larger than normal and that the baby's lungs were fully developed. Although it wasn't the ideal time to bring a baby into the world, he really didn't have a choice.

The sound of police sirens snapped J.R. out of his trance. He focused back on the road, only to notice the police was requesting for him to pull over. Traffic had slowed him down, so he knew that they couldn't have been stopping him for speeding. Wondering if he should risk it, seeing how the hospital was just a few feet ahead, J.R. decided to pull over, explain the situation, and take his ticket, so he could go about his business; but apparently, the officers had other plans.

"License and registration please?" the white officer requested as soon as J.R. rolled down the window.

He noticed his partner looking at his license plates before he joined them with his hand on his holster.

"Fuck y'all stopping me for?" J.R. asked as he retrieved the registration from the glove box.

"Shut up nigger! We asking the questions," Officer Friendly barked back.

"You better put an "A" at the end of "nigger" before we have bigger problems," J.R. threatened.

"Did you just threaten an officer? That's it. Out of the car," he ordered.

Pissed at himself for not keeping his mouth shut, J.R. did as they requested and got out. One of the officers searched him while the other officer searched the car. He knew they wasn't going to find shit, so he tried to keep his cool, just so they would let him go. The more he thought about not being there by Lexi side, the stronger his anger grew.

"Can y'all do what y'all gon' do so I can go?" J.R. asked but the look on the officer's face who was searching the car told another story.

"Well, would you look at what we have here," he said, causing his partner to turn around and J.R. to look closer.

J.R. squinted his eyes as he could not believe what the officer was pulling from under his passenger's seat. He knew what it looked like but knew damn well there was no way possible.

"Looks like we have one, two, three, four, five... six bricks right here." The officer smiled as he counted it aloud, sending J.R. immediately to a comatose state.

23

"THAT'S GAME NIGGA," COREY CHUCKLED AT THE EXPRESSION ON HIS COUSIN'S FACE

"I can't believe ya punk ass whoop my ass four games outta six," Mani tossed the controller on the table.

"Well believe it nigga," he chuckled.

Corey snatched his phone out his pocket, checking the time. It was going on ten o'clock and it had been couple of hours since Mari and J.R dipped. In the midst of placing his phone back in his pocket, it started vibrating in his hand. Noticing it was Mari, he answered quickly.

"Wassup, man?"

"I need y'all to meet me at the hospital. Something's wrong with Lexi and the baby and J.R ain't answering his phone," he said in panicked tone.

"He ain't answering his phone? I thought y'all rolled out together?" Corey asked while leaving out the basement to get Alyssa but caught her and Stasia walking out the front door.

"Man we were. Just hurry up and get here. We're at the same hospital Alyssa had her baby at."

"Aight. We're on our way."

"What the fuck is going on?" Mani asked, zipping up his hoodie.

"I'll explain in the car. We gotta go."

Assuming the kids were with the nanny, they dashed out the house into Mani whip. Corey filled him in on what was going on. When he mentioned that J.R. was M.I.A, Mani pulled out his cell phone and called him. After getting no answer, Mani placed the phone in the cup holder.

"What the fuck man? This nigga can't be missing right now. Not tonight of all nights! How the fuck did they end up getting separated?"

"Nigga ya guess is as good as mines. I told you what Mari told me."

Pushing the pedal to the floor, Mani did ninety the rest of the way to the hospital. Mani came to a screeching halt ten minutes later. They both hopped out the wheel, jogging inside the hospital where they saw his mother in-law, aunt, his wife, and sister in-law holding Drea back in the waiting area. Mari was rubbing his jaw and by how red it was, Corey knew Drea had laid hands on him.

"I can't believe y'all punk ass brother got *the audacity* to not fucking be here! Let something happen to my sister behind *his* bullshit. I swear on everything, I'ma kill his trifling ass!" Drea shouted while the women continued to hold her back.

"Y'all motherfuckas got the game *all* the way fucked up if y'all think y'all can play my nieces like this," Aunt Shirley pointed her finger at all of the men standing there.

The men looked back and forth between each other, speechless for a moment before Corey broke the ice.

"How is Lexi doing?"

"She's fine right now, but she'll be having the baby soon. Y'all need to find J.R. and get his ass here asap!" Drea spoke through gritted teeth.

The doctor called the Holiday family and informed them that Lexi was few centimeters dilated and estimated that she would be giving birth within an hour or so. Lysaa and Stasi glared at the men and without a word being said, they turned on their heels, heading towards the exit.

"Yo, what the fuck happened tonight?" Mani asked as soon as they got out of ear shot of everyone.

"I met up with that bitch Janice and J.R. and Kellz were with me. Janice was telling me some bullshit about Drea when she and Lexi rolled up on us. Drea swung on Janice, Lexi water broke, and she didn't wanna ride with J.R., so she rode with Drea. We were all following Drea and when we got here, that nigga didn't pull up."

Before anyone could say anything, Mari's phone rang.

Corey and Mani watched him on the phone. By the conversation along with the expression on his face, they knew it wasn't good.

"Just keep calm, man. I'll be there in a minute," he ended the call.

"Wassup?"

"J.R's in jail," Mari ran his hand over his head. "Somebody set him up. They found six bricks of cocaine in his whip and they trying to make that shit stick. I gotta go down there to see what the fuck they talking about," he ran to his car.

"We coming with you."

They hopped in Mani's ride and followed Mari to the precinct. Corey felt his pocket vibrate and retrieved his phone. He saw it was a number he didn't recognize but instead of ignoring the number, he answered.

"Who this?"

"It's Larry. Nigga we need to talk. Meet me in the back of the rehab. I'll be there waiting."

"I got something going on right now. I'll holla at you later," he tried to cut the conversation short.

"Nigga, if it wasn't important, I wouldn't be calling you. Meet me as soon as you can."

"Yo, drop me off at that rehab. I got something I need to handle."

"Nah. I'll roll with you. With the shit that happened tonight, we need to stick together. Let Mari know wassup."

Instead of arguing, Corey shot a text to Mari letting him that something came up that he needed to handle and that Mani was rolling with him. He shot a text back saying keep him posted and stuffed his phone in his pocket. His mind raced a mile a minute as they drove to the rehab. Corey hadn't talked to Larry since the night they were about to ride on Blue and, to be honest, he thought that was going to be his last time talking to him. Wondering how Larry got his number, he knew the only person that could've given it to him was Deana.

Parking at the end of the alley, Corey noticed a dark figure standing in the middle of alley. They both hopped out the car and headed down the alley where Larry stepped into the dim light. Larry's eyes instantly locked with Mani's, causing him to tense up. Corey noticed the change in his demeanor and held his hands up.

"It ain't what it seems like. This my family and he's interested in what you have to say," Corey looked between them. "So, wassup?"

"I see you took out Blue without me, huh?"

"That nigga had to be handled. Point, blank, period. Plus, that nigga was my problem for real. Not yours," Corey spat.

Larry nodded his head.

"Is that all you called me out here for?"

"Of course not. I just wanted to inform you that *another* one of our enemies was found killed a week or so in a motel room and niggas have been searching high and low for the niggas that did it," his eyes shifted between him and Mani.

"What the fuck that gotta do with us?" Mani asked, becoming pissed off.

"Come on now. Everybody know of the Rock Boyz and how they roll youngin'," Larry chuckled. "I just wanted to give y'all a heads up so when niggas in y'all camp come up missing, y'all know who's responsible."

"And who the fuck told you this? The same nigga that told you Blue was our common enemy?"

"As a matter of fact, it was. He keeps his ears to the street and he keeps me informed on all the relevant shit in the streets."

The stares between the men were intense and Corey was becoming angry; but instead of acting on his emotions, he decided it was time for them to roll. Turning to walk away, the cousins headed down the alley and hopped in the car. Mani pulled off down the block and headed towards I-285. Corey was reflecting on the conversation with Larry before his cousin interrupted his thoughts.

"Yo, I think we need have to kill that nigga and whoever else that's connected to him. That motherfucka and whoever else is working for him knows too much of our business, and I don't like that shit. And why did that nigga feel the need to tell you that shit anyway?"

"I don't know man, but something seemed off about him since he told me about that nigga Blue. I've been trying to figure out if that nigga is with us or against us. I just don't have proof of either."

"Everything comes at a price cuz. Remember that."

24

To say that things had been tense around the house was an understatement. Everybody seemed to be going through their own issues with the Holiday sisters. Although they were all keeping it together in front of the kids for the most part, everybody was pretty much going around and doing their own thing. D'Mani was just ready to get shit over with so that they could all go back to their respective homes, not that his troubles would end there anyway. He would still have to worry about the Cheyanne's situation.

Anastasia had truly surprised him. Though she wasn't being friendly to Cheyanne by any means, she wasn't being as evil as he knew she was capable of being. He was assuming that had more to do with the fact that *she* was rocking his ring and less to do with her being sympathetic to the girl; but he would take whatever he could get. At least she wasn't being stingy with the pussy; even though he knew she was still upset with him, that in itself took some of the stress off of him.

D'Mani looked over at Stasia as she slept beside him and

decided that he wouldn't wake her since she seemed to be so peaceful right then. He had to take Cheyanne to see her doctor since she had to get checked out every week. Slowly, he climbed out of the bed so that the movement wouldn't disturb her and headed to the bathroom. He set the shower to the temperature he liked and stripped out of his boxer briefs before stepping inside and under the warm flow of water. As he reached for his soap, there was a knock at the door and Stasia's voice was the next thing he heard.

"What you doin' up so early?" she asked. He noted that it wasn't a hint of attitude in her voice. When he peaked outside of the glass shower door, he saw that she was using the toilet, so he surmised that she hadn't followed him in there on some bullshit. However, he couldn't say that it wouldn't be a problem after she found out where he was going.

"Uhh, Cheyanne got a doctor's appointment. I was going to run her there real quick." He let her know and waited for the shit to hit the fan. Stasia remained quiet as she flushed and took her time washing her hands before pulling the shower door open and giving him the look of death.

"Really? Don't she got an aid or something that can do that shit? You've already done more than enough for her already D'Mani. You gotta go to her appointments with her now too?" D'Mani released a deep sigh. He really wasn't trying to go back and forth with her about Cheyanne, especially when Stasia would take that as him taking up for her.

"I already told you Stasia that I'm just doing this because she's the mother of my child man... the girl ain't got nobody! Not one person! The least I can do is support her before she dies!" he was tired of saying the same shit to her over and over again, but it seemed like she was going to feel however she wanted to feel about the situation; however, that wasn't going to change his stance. And he wasn't going to leave Cheyanne to fend for herself just to appease Stasia.

"Okay well then, I'll come too since she needs so much support!" she huffed with a raised brow like she was just waiting for him to object.

"Cool, now can you close the door so I can finish my shower." He turned back around so that he could continue washing up before they ended up being late. Being petty, she left the bathroom without doing what he asked, initiating him to curse under his breath.

Ten minutes later, D'Mani stepped out of the shower and brushed his teeth quickly before stepping out of the bathroom, releasing a cloud of steam with him. Silently, Anastasia brushed past him and slamming the door behind her. He couldn't help but chuckle at her childish ass. He continued to his closet and pulled out a pair of black joggers with a red and black Jordan shirt and his "gym red" Jordan's. After slipping on a black hoodie, he was ready to go. A knock at the door stopped him from going to rush Stasia's ass, and he made a beeline to see who it was.

"Hey, I was just trying to see if you were ready," Cheyanne said once he opened the door.

"Hey daddy!" Imani bounced beside her, already dressed and ready to go.

"Good morning Princess Imani," he greeted her and bent down to give her a kiss. "We'll be ready in a second."

"We?" The look on Cheyanne's face showed her confusion.

"Yes we." D'Mani hadn't even heard Anastasia come out of the bathroom, but she stood beside him in her towel still wet from the shower.

"Oh okaaaay," Cheyanne dragged, looking between the two of them before grabbing Imani's hand and walking off down the hall. As soon as her back was turned, Anastasia smacked her lips and went back into the room to get dressed.

"You ain't have to do all that," D'Mani said once the door was closed.

"Do all of what?" she feigned confusion as she walked about the room naked, gathering her stuff to get dressed.

"Nothin' man," he sighed and headed out of the room. "We leavin' in ten minutes." He let her know and slammed the door before she could say anything.

Twenty minutes later, they were all in the truck and headed to the doctor's office. Anastasia made sure to take her sweet ass time getting dressed and made them late just to throw on a fucking pair of jeans and a sweatshirt. Besides her being extra as fuck for making them run late, she was being overly affectionate but *only* when she felt like Cheyanne was paying attention. If the girl wasn't around then her ass was giving him icy stares and being sarcastic. The whole car ride, D'Mani had to refrain from shrugging her off of him because she was damn near leaned all the way over into his seat.

When they finally pulled into the parking lot, he hurried and got out so that he could get Imani out of her car seat. He wasn't even going to entertain Anastasia's bullshit, so he walked Imani over to the entrance to wait for her mother and Stasia to get out instead of opening the door for them like he normally would have. Cheyanne was already standing next to them by the time Anastasia realized that he wasn't going to get her door, and she was clearly pissed; but he wasn't going to be played with.

"You could have opened the door for me D'Mani!" she huffed, stepping onto the elevator behind them.

"I could've," he shrugged. He let Imani press the button for the fifth floor and tried to ignore the evil glare that Stasia was throwing his way. She was acting like a straight brat and he didn't have time for that childish shit. Besides them having sex that one time, Cheyanne hadn't given Anastasia a reason to suspect that she was on any bullshit with him. He thought that him making the leap to propose would further put her at ease, but it was obvious that it hadn't.

The elevator finally dinged, letting them off on the floor of the clinic, and Cheyanne, who had been pressed against the back wall, rushed to get off before anyone else. She led the way to the unit that they needed to go to and he, Imani, and Stasia trailed behind her. D'Mani couldn't help but to look around at all of the elderly people who were there to see a cardiologist, and wonder how something that to his knowledge only affected old people. had managed to touch his family. He shook his head at the thought and took a seat in the half crowded waiting room. Since they had cut the time so close, the nurse came out and called Cheyanne's name before she even got a chance to sit down. D'Mani thought about going in the back with her but decided against it since he had Imani. Instead, he stayed in his seat and let her play games on his phone while Anastasia huffed and puffed behind him. He ignored her the entire time and gave all of his attention to his baby girl, hoping that at some point Anastasia would realize how dumb her behavior was.

Cheyanne's appointment ended up being an hour or so long. When she finally reentered the waiting area, D'Mani could tell that she'd been crying even though she'd done a fairly good job at hiding it. He immediately stood up and met her with questioning eyes.

"You okay? What the hell they say back there?" he knew those were stupid questions to ask somebody who had already been diagnosed with a terminal illness, but she had seemed alright before she'd went in. What more could a doctor tell someone that *knew* they were dying to make them cry.

"Yes, I'm fine... I'm just ready to go. I'm just tired," she lied, stepping around him and walking towards the elevators. Imani was still sitting in her chair completely engrossed in some damn video, but Anastasia was already standing at the elevators with her shades on like they were on her time. D'Mani helped Imani down and they made their way down to where the two ladies stood. He caught the end of their conversation.

"Look, I'm not asking you to like me because if I was you, I probably would have a problem with me too, but I am asking that you *stop* with the bullshit. I'm *not* here for D'Mani. I'm here trying to spend the little bit of time I have left with *my baby* before I fuckin' *cease* to exist! I'd like to think that is *more important* than your petty ass beef, but if it's not too much to ask, please refrain from sayin' stupid shit to me." Cheyanne hissed before clearing her throat once she realized he was standing there and then stepped onto the elevator. The look on Anastasia's face showed her surprise, and D'Mani hoped that she'd take heed to what Cheyanne said.

They climbed on after Cheyanne, giving her space to sort through whatever she had been told by the doctor. D'Mani couldn't help but to feel bad about not going back with her because it was clear that she wasn't going to tell him what was said. He would just wait and call the doctor himself once they got back to the house, *if* Anastasia didn't try and pick a fight with him about whatever had just happened.

25

Hearing the faint cries from his newborn son almost brought tears to J.R.'s eyes. Considering the fucked-up circumstances he was in, he had to find light somewhere at the end of the tunnel. Within a matter of months, he lost his mother and little sister. The one and only thing he had looked forward to was the birth of his son, and he wasn't even present for that. Life was beginning to take a toll on him, and if it wasn't for Lexi and the baby, he probably would have been clocked out.

"Oh my God J.R., he looks just like you," Drea's voice beamed through the phone.

"Can Lexi talk yet? Let me talk to her," he requested.

J.R. waited for a response from Drea but instead, he heard Lexi's soft, tired voice.

"Baby, you good?" he asked, eyeing the other men in the room who waited to use the phone.

"I can't believe you not here," she cried, breaking his heart into small pieces.

"I know baby. I know. Stop crying though. Stasia recorded everything and I swear to God when I'm out this bitch, I'll never leave y'all side again," he promised, meaning every single word.

"Ok," she sniffled, which eased his mind a briefly.

"What happened? You were right behind us," she continued.

"They pulled me over for some bullshit that I don't need you stressing over. I need you to be healthy for our son. Matter fact, let me talk to my shorty," he said, smiling once he heard Lexi chuckle.

"Well, he's busy right now. Just handle whatever it is you have to handle and get home to us," she pleaded.

"Bet. I love y'all."

"We love you too baby."

J.R. ended the call and placed the receiver back on the hook before going back to the round table. Once there, he placed his face inside the palm of both hands. He couldn't believe the luck he was having. Missing the birth of his son had him feeling like the worst person in world. The reason for his absence was some bullshit and whoever was behind it was going to pay with their life.

"You good young blood?" he heard a deep voice say from over his shoulder.

J.R. looked up and noticed an older man with a salt and pepper beard standing behind him. At first, he thought about ignoring him but that could go one or two ways and beating that old man's ass was not part of the plans.

"I'm straight," he finally replied after trying to feel him out first.

The older gentleman gave him a head nod and walked away. He wasn't even gone two minutes before a fight broke out. J.R. remained seated and watched the rest of *Judge Judy* on the old box television while the other inmates ran towards the chaos. The door buzzed loudly, indicating that the correctional officers were on their way in. J.R. glanced over as they tried to break things up, eventually making everyone go inside their cell.

"You know they finna lock us in right?" his temporary roommate Motor stated as soon as the bars locked.

J.R. didn't bother replying to him because he talked too much. He had only been booked a few hours yet, he knew the man's life story. Niggas like him had to be fed with a long handle spoon simply because they ran their mouth like bitches.

"You get in touch with ya girl?" Motor asked as he climbed onto the top bunk.

"Yeah." J.R. replied drily, hoping Motor took the hint.

Apparently, he did because no more questions were asked and he was sound asleep, snoring. J.R. took that opportunity and silence to get his mind right. He hadn't been able to process the fact that the bricks were in his car and he knew he wasn't the one who placed them there. His mind had been so occupied with Lexi and the baby, he hadn't processed the fact that he had been set up.

Thinking back to the events of that day, he wondered who had *the time* to set him up. He wrecked his brain until it *finally* hit him. When him, Mari, Kellz, and Janice were at the restaurant, Kellz excused herself. She told J.R. that she must have dropped her lip gloss in his car and wanted to go get it. Thinking about the possibility of Lexi finding it instead, he tossed her his keys and urged her to go find her shit. She must have used that time to plant the bricks but why?

J.R. started to reflect on the different encounters he had with Kellz and found nothing fishy about her. What blew his mind even more was that she was recommended by his own blood, Julian. *Was Julian in on the bullshit too? What was Kellz motive?* All those thoughts plagued his mind, but he knew he wouldn't be able to get any answers from where he was.

Letting out a long frustrating sigh, J.R. pounded his fist

on the hard bed and stood to his feet. He walked over to the bars where he called out for a correctional officer.

"GUARD!" he screamed out, trying to be heard amongst the other men screaming.

A woman correctional officer was already headed in his direction, so she stopped and just stared at him.

"I need to make a call," he advised her.

"I don't care what you need to do," she replied before walking off.

"FAT PIGEON- TOED ASS BITCH!" He yelled out to her, but she never turned around.

"We on lockdown bro. We won't be using no phones probably until tomorrow, if we lucky." Motor woke up out of his sleep and informed him before his snores filled the small cell again.

"Ain't this a bitch. I need to get in touch with the guys. They need to get ahold of Julian and Kellz, asap." He cursed to himself before laying down on the hard steel.

26

Since the night of J.R's arrest, shit around the house had been more tense than normal. With J.R. being absent during the birth of his son mixed with the hell the Holiday sisters were already giving their men, it seemed they asses couldn't catch a break. When one fucked up, they *all* fucked up, and Corey felt like he was catching it the worse. He'd been trying to plead his case to Alyssa about Deana for days, but she wasn't trying to hear that shit. Corey explained that the relationship between him and shawty was innocent and that he never laid a finger on her ass, but Alyssa didn't give a fuck. The fact that he had another bitch basically *taking care* of him while he was in rehab didn't sit right with her. Her argument was that he could've had any damn body in the family handling business for him since she couldn't due to the pregnancy; but the fact that he had picked a *random* hoe to be in his business had Alyssa in her feelings. Understanding where his wife was coming from, Corey apologized every chance he got, but it meant nothing.

Waking up to an empty bed, Corey felt around for his phone and checked the time. It was a few minutes before eleven, so he decided to get his ass up. After washing and getting dressed in a grey Nike sweat suit and matching color J's, he straightened up their room and grabbed his phone before leaving the room. Heading down the stairs, he went straight to the kitchen where the Holiday sisters were talking but when they saw him, they became mute, giving him the death stare.

"What you want?" Lexi snapped.

"Lyssa, I'm about to run our real quick. Do you want me to bring you anything back?"

"Nothing I can think of at the moment but if I think of something, I'll text you," she answered in a soft voice.

Corey could tell by the redness of her eyes that she'd been crying and that shit hurt his heart. They stared at each other for few more seconds before he backed out of the kitchen doorway and headed out the front door, hopping inside his truck. Pulling out of the driveway, Corey hopped on the expressway with his music blasting and his mind focused on one person, Larry. The conversation they had in the alley that night had been playing in his nonstop and it was bugging the fuck out of him. When Larry took it upon himself to introduce himself to Corey, he thought that the nigga was being cool with him just because. However, the more he analyzed the situation and how things played out between them, the suspicions that Corey had about Larry intensified. The nigga knew *too much* information about him, his brothers, and the moves they were making. Most of the niggas that worked for them came here from New York, and it didn't make sense for them to give up information on them to nigga that couldn't do shit for them. Even though Corey wanted to rule out the fact that one of the day ones was running their mouth, he couldn't shake the feeling that someone close to them was living foul.

Parking in the nearest spot forty minutes later, he hopped

out his truck and headed inside the rehab. He looked around the waiting area and it was the same way it was when Corey checked himself in a few months back. The fiends looked like something out of the *Thriller* video. He cringed from the sight and had a good mind to leave, but he was there on business. Signing in at the front desk, the nurse looked at the name, gave him a smile, and told him he could go back. Bending the corner, he saw Larry finishing up a conversation he was having with a young dude that looked to be around his age. Corey sized the nigga up as he passed him before focusing on Larry.

"What's good youngin'? I never thought that you would step foot in this motherfucka again," Larry chuckled. "You here to see me?"

"Yeah. I figured I come chop it up with you for a minute," Corey smirked.

"Step inside."

They walked into his room and Larry closed the door before taking a seat across from Corey.

"What's on ya mind man?"

"To be honest, it seems you know more about *me* than I know about *you* my nigga and your generosity towards me has me a little curious."

"Oh, so you figure because I gave you a heads up about Blue and I know about your camp, you feel like I'm up to something," he nodded his head slowly.

"Niggas don't do shit out of the kindness of their hearts these days old head," Corey spat.

"See, that's where you're wrong. Old heads like me try to look out for young, dumb niggas like you who think they got this street shit figured out but don't know shit for real. The info I gave was to let you know that somebody is heavily *watching* y'all and for y'all to move more carefully. I done had my run at the streets. I done seen the highs and lows of the shit. Yeah, I had the bitches, cars, nice houses, and niggas I thought that was gonna ride with me until I was in the ground; but that shit ruined my life and now I'm in here. I apologize that my notions made ya ass suspicious. So from now on, I'll keep my info to myself," Larry turned his back on him.

Corey sat there a few seconds staring at the back of Larry's head. He chuckled at the old head's speech Larry had just preached, but he didn't by that shit for one minute. He believed the part about him being in the streets but that shit about him looking out for the so called *young, dumb niggas,* that was the bullshit Corey wasn't buying. Instead of asking anymore questions, he got up and left without saying a word. Exiting the rehab, he popped the locks to his truck and was about to hop inside until he heard a female call his name. Turning around, Corey saw Deana jogging towards him.

"Damn. You just gonna roll out without speaking to me? I thought we were better than that Corey."

"I guess not," he shrugged.

"Really? You just gonna treat me like this after what I did for ya ass?"

"Look I appreciate all you did for me Deana, but that shit is *over with*. I'm not in rehab no more. So whatever you used to do for me, I can do on my own. You cool peoples shawty, but we *can't* have *no type* of relationship outside of this. I have a wife and kid and that's my focus right now. I ain't got no time for you," Corey answered nonchalantly.

Not giving her a chance to respond, he hopped in his truck and pulled off, heading home. Upon entering the mansion, Corey went straight to the basement where he knew his cousins were. Walking into a cloud of weed smoke, he took a seat in one of the recliner chairs.

"Wassup cuz? Where was you?" Mani asked before hitting the blunt.

"I went to go holla at the nigga Larry. Tryna find out the reason behind him giving me info I didn't ask for."

"And his response was?" Mari inquired.

"He said he was just trying to look out for me and let me know that we were being heavily watched and to move with more caution," Corey huffed.

"Do you believe him?"

"I don't believe none of that shit. I thought for a moment that someone on the inside could be leaking shit, but what would they have to gain from that? The nigga can't offer them shit."

His cousins nodded their heads in agreement.

"I think the nigga that was there with him when I got there might know something though."

"What nigga?" Mani passed the blunt to his brother.

"Some tall, brown skin nigga with waves. He was one of them *pretty boy* types."

The ringing of the door bell interrupted their conversation. Being closest to the basement door, Corey was the first one up the steps. Answering the door, he balled his fist up at the sight of the nigga before him.

"Yo Corey? Who at the door?" Mari called out behind him.

"*This* the nigga right here!"

27

"Wh...what's up fellas? What y'all talkin' bout?" Julian stuttered and looked away from Corey.

"We talkin' bout *you*... you just left from talking to Larry. How you know him?" Corey stepped towards Julian and Mari stepped in between them.

He studied the faces of each of the guys that were present and something was off. Julian had stepped in when Corey went away and there hadn't been any major problems, but Mari could tell that there was about to some issues in the near future. Mari knew that Corey felt some type of way and felt like he had been replaced, which couldn't have been further from the truth. Business was business and he was happy that his cousin stepped up and got himself together so that things could be back to normal. He thought about how J.R. had gotten jammed up and thought about Julian because they hadn't seen him in a couple of days. So him showing up at that very moment put Mari's mind at ease; at least for the time being.

"Say Julian... how do you know *this Larry* cat?" Mari quizzed.

"That's my Uncle man..." Julian replied as he fumbled with his phone.

"I gotta go y'all... family emergency," Julian said and dipped out before anyone could say anything.

"That nigga *lying*... I *know* he's lying. He hates that I'm back home *and* he on some funny shit," Corey fumed.

Mari was about to respond, but his phone rang. It was the call that he had been waiting on, so he excused himself and answered.

"Give me some good news Benny... it's been long enough," Mari got right to the point.

He listened as Benny ran down the details and finally smiled for the first time in a couple of days.

"That's no problem. I'm sure my wife can handle that or she can find someone who will... yeah... aight... thanks man. I owe ya," Mari hung up.

"Aye y'all... I'm headed downtown to pick J.R. up. They been fuckin' around wit his phone calls and shit, but my mans got everything straight and I can bond him out. I'll be back in a few," Mari told Mani and Corey as he left.

The bitch ass cops had been playing with J.R. long enough, and D'Mari was thankful that Benny was finally able to pull some strings. He rode in silence with a mind full of thoughts, en route to picking up his bruh. Mari didn't give Mani nor Corey the option to ride because the police station was the *very last* place that the four of them needed to be seen together. If Lexi hadn't just given birth, Mari would have made her pick him up. But since he was the most level headed out of the crew, he did it.

Forty minutes later, he parked and paid and then made his way inside. He was about to see just how much rank Benny had because the *only* thing he told him to do was walk in and write J.R.'s name down and *not* say *one* word while inside. Mari did just that and ten minutes and countless death stares later,

J.R. walked out. Mari saw that he was getting ready to say something, so he motioned for him to wait, and they both exited without saying shit. As soon as they got inside of Mari's vehicle, J.R. let all of his frustrations out.

"FUCCKKK!!!" he roared, hitting the dash board.

Mari didn't even say shit because he was sure that it had been a rough few days for his homie. He was pissed off himself because they had been giving him the run around. As soon as they were a safe distance away, Mari pulled a backwood out of the console and handed it to J.R. He normally didn't even allow smoking in his shit, but he knew it was needed at that moment.

"Imma kill that muthafuckin' bitch and Imma kill my bitch ass cousin too!" J.R. declared.

"Speaking of yo cousin... Corey saw him talking to that cat Larry that he's been getting info from. Suddenly, he popped up today and dipped right out. He said Larry is his uncle," Mari explained.

"Uncle? Uncle? That nigga ain't got *no muthafuckin' uncle* so that further confirms him and that bitch behind that shit. Take me to my crib... we gotta handle some shit," J.R. said.

"You mean yo crib crib?" Mari queried.

"Yeah... then I got one more stop Imma need to make then we can go back to the house."

"You ain't ready to see your new baby *and* your girl?"

"I am, but I gotta handle some shit or I ain't gon' be able to rest. Just let me have this one man. Where your phone charger so I can check a location right quick?"

Mari handed J.R. his phone charger and continued navigating towards their destination. Mari hadn't been to J.R.'s place since the shooting. That day had changed all of their lives for the worst and shit hadn't looked right since then. Mari knew that everyone was in a hurry to get back to their regular lives, but he knew that patience was a virtue. He didn't mind the temporary transition because it would only ensure long term freedom. He had another thing to present to the family that he was sure was going to cause a big uproar, but it was going to be done within the next few weeks. Mari knew that it was going to be out of the question for the women to leave, but it was time for the older women in the family and the babies to leave for a while. Mississippi seemed like the best place for them and he hoped that the Holiday sisters didn't act a fool. If they did, they could go as well, but he knew that would be too much like right.

Mari pulled up to J.R.'s house and J.R. didn't waste any time getting out. Mari got out and checked their surroundings just to be on the safe side. He had an idea of what J.R. was about to do, and he couldn't blame him. D'Mari heard his phone ringing, so he hopped back in the truck and answered it. The January weather was cool. It wasn't as cold as New York, but chilly nonetheless. Mari talked to Mani for a few minutes and listened as he told him about some shit that was going on at one of the traps. He put his hands on his temples and massaged them as he thought about how it was *always* some bullshit going on. Mani was pissed the fuck off and D'Mari knew what was coming soon without him even having to say it.

A few minutes later, J.R. jogged out of the house and jumped in wearing all black. Mari knew that he probably was happy to take a shower, but deep down he knew that was only gonna make Lexi cuss his ass out even more. He had missed the birth of their son and then didn't come straight to see them.

"Go to this address right here. I know Julian's bitch ass on the run if he dipped out like you said, but I'm pretty sure I can catch that bitch there," J.R. asserted.

It was fifteen minutes after seven when Mari pulled up to the address that J.R. had given him. He killed the engine and checked his waist for his nine because he knew what was about to go down.

"I got it man... you ain't even gotta..."

"Shut up nigga. You know I got ya back," Mari cut J.R. off and they both got out.

Mari listened as J.R. gave him a heads up on what to expect. He explained that he had used an app and texted from Julian's number, hoping that Kellz fell for the shit. J.R. didn't wanna be on no sneak type shit. As soon as they made it to the door, J.R. knocked and as soon as the locks clicked, they both pulled their guns out just to be ready.

"Nigga I thought you dipped out on..."

"He did bitch!" J.R. gritted his teeth and pushed his gun into Kellz's forehead.

"I... I ca... I can explain," Kellz stuttered.

"Oh you wanna explain how *you* and *my cousin* set my ass up... if that ain't what you explaining, you can just shut the fuck up," J.R. spat.

"I owe Julian my life J.R. I'm really sorry. He would've killed me if I didn't..."

POP!"

J.R. sent a bullet right between Kellz's eyes, ending her sob story.

"Damn you shoulda let her keep talkin' to see what all she knew," Mari said.

"Fuck that bitch... call them people."

"Text already sent. Now come on and let me get you home so Lexi can beat your ass!" Mari chuckled.

28

After the shit at the doctor's office, D'Mani made sure to keep Cheyanne and Stasia apart, not that it was an easy task since they all lived in the same house. The constant one-sided pettiness was even more irritating since they were all dealing with some much more serious shit than Anastasia feeling threatened by Cheyanne's presence. He was more than happy when he told D'Mari that there was some shit he needed to handle at one of the traps. He was fed up being around the estrogen that had taken over the house. There were babies, hormones, and feelings all over that big muthafucka and putting in some real work would definitely make him feel like his old self again, at least he hoped so anyway.

He went and peeked into the room that Cheyanne and Imani were in, noticing that they were both sleeping. Cheyanne had been spending all of her time cooped up in the room since Anastasia had been making her feel less than welcome, and baby girl had been laid up under her almost like she knew something wasn't right with her mother. D'Mani had told her after the doctor's appointment that they needed to talk to Imani and explain what was going on. He could tell by the way she tensed up that the last thing she was ready to do was tell their daughter that she was going to heaven. He totally sympathized with her; he just wished Anastasia did too.

D'Mani closed the door back quietly and headed downstairs. He was on his way to handle a money issue the only way it could be done, by laying a nigga to rest. As many enemies as the Roc Boyz had, they couldn't afford to leave any loose strings.

"Where you goin'?"

The sound of Anastasia's voice literally caused him to pause mid-step. D'Mani hadn't known where she was in the house, but he wasn't expecting to run into her before he left for his mission. He needed his mind right to handle the task and arguing with her was sure to fuck up his whole vibe. His first instinct was to keep going and avoid the confrontation that was sure to come, but that would just make shit worse.

"I got somethin' to handle, I'll be back soon." He continued to the door, ignoring the grunt that she released at his response. There was no reason for her to have an attitude. Cheyanne was upstairs, so it wasn't like he was sneaking out to meet a bitch. That nasty tone she'd used was some mind games. She probably figured that guilt for making her suspicious of him would stop him from leaving... shit it had in the past, but right then was something totally different! D'Mani wasn't going to let her fuck up the adrenaline high he was on.

After he got into his car, he blasted his Future mixtape the whole way to the Vine City where the thievin' ass nigga Ty lived. You would think he would be feeling a certain way considering that he was about to take somebody's life, but D'Mani was calmer than he'd been the last few weeks. He had to admit that he was probably ready to take out his frustrations on somebody, and it didn't bother him at all that it would be Ty.

Once he got to English Avenue, he slowed down his speed and began creeping so that he could make sure he had the right address. D'Mani knew the nigga's schedule and had planned on catching him before he even made it to the steps of his raggedy ass apartment building. Noticing that he still hadn't pulled up, D'Mani parked a few houses away and sparked up a blunt while he waited. He was surprised at the nigga's boldness. Any smart person would have run if they were going to steal some shit. However, Ty must have thought that they were all so busy dealing with their beef that they wouldn't notice some petty money being stolen. Little did he know, D'Mani didn't give a fuck if it was a crumb. If it belonged to him and his family, it was off limits. Also, it was already a slap in the face for his ass to feel the need to steal considering that D'Mani, D'Mari, JR, and Corey paid their guys well. If there was something that he needed, Ty knew he could have come to them and asked and more than likely, he would have gotten it. Now though, there wasn't shit he could ask for but a quick and painless death, and he'd better hope that D'Mani was willing to grant it for him.

Not even five minutes after he'd smashed the rest of his blunt out in the ashtray, he saw Ty's beat up Buick pulling into the only empty spot in front of his building. D'Mani sat straight up in his seat and pulled out his Glock, waiting for Ty to step outside of his car so that he could run up on him. When the nigga finally stepped foot out of his car, Ty damn near fell and laughed out loud at himself. It was obvious his ass was drunk. Shaking his head, D'Mani climbed out of his car as well and crept alongside the other cars parked on the curb. He watched Ty stagger his way across the street, towards where he sat hunched down in irritation. Call him crazy, but Mani didn't feel like he should have been waiting the twenty damn minutes it was taking to send his ass to hell or where ever the fuck he was gone go.

The silence on the block aided to the crime he was about to commit as he came from behind the fleet of cars with his gun drawn just as Ty slipped and landed dead on his face on the side walk. D'Mani released a low whistle and bent down so that he could speak directly into his ear.

"That shit looked like it hurt nigga. Stand yo stupid ass up so you can catch this bullet and I can go home." He hissed. Ty immediately threw his hands up and let out a low growl as he lazily climbed to his feet.

"Y'all niggas the stupid ones." He slurred. "It took y'all this long to figure out I *been* skimmin' off yo packs!" he spit out blood on the ground and grinned widely. D'Mani hit him with an uppercut, causing his teeth to clatter together and him to double over in pain.

"You think it's *funny* that you bout to *die* over the type of money me and my brothers wipe our asses with? We gotta start makin' niggas fill out applications and shit cause y'all niggas embarrassin' as fuck! Anyway, at least you gone be with yo family where you goin'." D'Mani shrugged, releasing two bullets into his head just as he went to react. He really ain't have no intentions on going in the house and killing the nigga's mama and girlfriend. He just wanted to fuck with his head before he aired his shit out. Tucking his gun back in his jeans, D'Mani looked around his environment, even though he knew that the silencer had stopped anybody from suspecting what had just happened, before coolly walking back to his truck. He sent a quick text to his brother once he was a safe distance away, letting him know that it was done, almost receiving an instant reply back of a simple "Bet."

On the way home, D'Mani stopped by Proctor Creek to get rid of his gun before heading back home to fuck the attitude right out of Anastasia.

29

Amir Johan Ratcliff was the biggest blessing J.R. had ever received. Although he wasn't there for his actual birth, he planned on making it up to his son throughout life. Being home was a gift and a curse within itself. Their house was full of arguing couples, crying ass newborns, active ass toddlers, a dying baby momma, and an aunt who was supposed to be there to help out, but she didn't do shit but smoke all their weed.

As far as the streets were concerned, nothing had changed over the days. Julian was still missing. He even disconnected the number they had on him and checked out days ago from the hotel he was last staying at. J.R. thought about hitting up some of his homies from Philly to see if they've seen him. Julian knew better to stay in Atlanta, so J.R. was pretty sure he was headed back East.

It had been about a week or so since the last time J.R. checked on Jessica. She was still at the trap house and being tended to, but J.R. needed to make his move on Grant Tessa; therefore, he needed to holler at her ASAP.

Finishing up his bottle of water at the kitchen table, J.R. stood up, tossed it in the trash, and headed downstairs where the guys were. J.R. made it to the bottom of the steps and peeked his head around the corner. D'Mani was smoking a blunt on the couch while Mari and Corey were engaged in an intense game of pool.

"Aye, I'll be back, I'm about to make a run. Gotta holler at Jessica." He announced, turning around and heading back up the flight of stairs.

"AYYYYEEEEE J.R.!" Mari called out loudly, causing him to pause in his tracks.

"Wad up?" J.R. yelled downstairs without turning around.

"Mannnn.... Come here." Mari said this time, causing J.R. to shake his head.

Slowly turning around, he dragged himself back down the stairs into the sitting area, where they all were now. J.R. stopped far away from them, close enough to the stairs yet close enough to still engage with them.

"Man, what the fuck y'all want?" he asked, twisting his head to the side.

"We need to holler at you about something. Chill." Corey finally chimed in.

"Ain't this a bitch. Y'all finna have an intervention for me, like we did this nigga months ago?" J.R. replied, pointing to Corey.

"Man sit yo bitch ass down." D'Mari laughed, causing everyone else to chuckle as well.

Not really having time to waste but wanting to hear his homies out, J.R. decided to give them five minutes.

"Aight. Gon' kick the shit off." He huffed, walking over and taking a seat on the armrest of the couch.

D'Mari wasted no time speaking up first.

"You need to chill out."

"Exactly. You running around this motherfucker like a chicken with its head cut off." Mani stated.

"Right. You got a brand-new baby up there. This street shit ain't going nowhere." Corey added in.

J.R. listened as they took turns chewing him out. He knew that they were only telling him what he needed to hear. J.R. hadn't been the same since the war began. He had taken so many losses that he didn't have time to stop and just let shit happen. He had to take action in his own hands and now that his son was here, he really had to kill this shit before it killed him.

"Aight. I'm hearing y'all. Let me go make this run real quick and then I'll slow down eventually." J.R. replied, standing to his feet and walking towards the stairs.

He could hear each of them huff and puff behind his back but none of them was dealing with half the shit he was dealing one; therefore, they didn't understand.

"SO JUST FUCK WHAT WE SAID HUH?" he heard Mani yell out, but he had already made his mind up and *nothing and no one* was changing that.

J.R. eased his way up the stairs and through the kitchen. He stopped at the refrigerator and grabbed another bottle of water before officially heading out. He almost made it to the door when he heard sniffles and whispers coming from the lower level bathroom. The door was practically open, but Lexi's sisters' backs were towards him. Stepping a little closer, he noticed they were huddled around Lexi, who was sitting on the edge of the tub crying. J.R. tuned out everything else around him and listened closely.

"Lexi, I know J.R. loves you, we all know that man loves you." Alyssa spoke first.

"There's a difference between *loving me* and knowing *how to* love me." She sobbed.

"These streets..... I'm scared that I'm going to lose him. Look at us. We ain't no hood bitches, but now all we do is *bald-headed hoe* shit." Lexi continued, causing all her sisters to laugh.

"But for real y'all. I've made up my mind. I'm taking the baby and moving back to Mississippi." Lexi said, breaking down this time.

J.R.'s heart wouldn't allow him to listen anymore. He turned around and headed up the stairs towards the bedroom. Walking passed the nursery, he heard soft cries. Glancing inside, he noticed Corey's daughter crib empty, so he turned the corner slightly and peeped Amir stirring in his sleep.

A smile crept across J.R.'s face as he went to pick up his boy. Amir began crying but stopped as soon as his small beady eyes focused on his dad.

"You hungry my manz." J.R. said as he began to rock Amir.

He still was amazed at the fact that he was a father. Amir had all of his features and Lexi's light brown complexion. He took his son and walked over to the rocking chair that wasn't far from his crib. J.R. grabbed one of Lexi's breast milk bottles from the stand. He tested it, assuring that it was room temperature how he liked it, took a seat, and started to feed his son. Although Amir's eyes closed with every slurp, J.R. still stared into them. He was going to make everything right, starting with his family.

After Amir finished up his six ounce bottle, J.R .burped him before carefully placing him back in his bed. He stood over him momentarily and patted his back to ensure he was good. Slowly easing up, J.R. turned around and ran into Lexi.

"I- I- I -I thought you was gone." She stuttered and fidgeted in front of him.

"Nah. I'm here." He stared at her in the eyes.

J.R. pulled Lexi closer to him by her small waist, never breaking eye contact with his lady.

"You think one of them would watch him while we go make a run?" He asked, pecking her on the lips.

Lexi looked at him confused before shaking her head up and down. It was obvious that J.R. had caught her off guard.

"Where we going?" she quizzed.

"To get married." He said nonchalantly, breaking his hold and walking away.

"TO WHAT?!" she screamed out, clearly forgetting where she was.

"Y'all wake him up. I ain't watching him." Aunt Shirley said as J.R. walked passed her while Lexi ran through the hallway trying to catch up to him.

Once inside their bedroom, J.R. grabbed his Nike Air Force Ones out of the closet. He sat on the bed and began putting them on while Lexi stood in the doorway staring at him.

"Where you going?" she asked, placing her hand on her hip.

"*To marry you*. Can you get dressed please? They close in a few hours." He urged her.

Lexi looked on and busted out in laughter but stopped, noticing she was the only one laughing.

"Wait. You serious?" she walked closer and asked.

J.R. stood to his feet and pulled her in close to his chest.

"I'm *dead ass*......Lexi, ain't nobody else out here for me man. I love you and I want you to be my wife.... *Officially*."

Instead of replying, Lexi stepped back and looked him over as if she was trying to figure him out.

"I ain't got no ring or no shit, but I knew since day one you would become *my wife*. I just didn't know when, so of course, this wasn't planned." He said honestly.

"GET THE FUCK OUTTA HERE!" she screamed, jumping up and down.

"Just say *yeah* girl..... DAMN!" he laughed.

"Yes.... Yes.... Yes.... I'll be your wife!" She squirmed, jumping in his arms.

30

After being home for a few weeks, Corey had ease himself back into the streets. Finding out that Julian tried to frame J.R. and dealing with niggas with sticky fingers, he felt like he needed to be back in the swing of things. Since he'd been operating with a clear head and was free of all intoxicating substances, Corey was ready to get back to dealing with the day to day operations. Once he was back on the scene, the workers inquired about his absence, but instead of giving them the long story, he kept it simple by saying that he needed time to get his shit together. The trap houses were still operating like normal and the when he learned the truck's schedule, Corey made sure shit was flowing the way that it should.

Although he was familiarizing himself with the streets again, Corey, as well as the rest of his brothers, still tried to make time for their families. However, it seemed like the harder he tried to make things right with Alyssa, the more she pushed him away. She managed to lose her attitude and was being more cordial with him but his wife was being *stingy* with pussy. It was one thing to wait four to six weeks for her to heal from giving birth, but for her to *purposely* withhold sex from him was downright cruel in his eyes; but instead of bitching about it, Corey just took it on the chin but planned to end that shit soon.

"Alana, baby, can you please stop crying?" Corey heard Alyssa pleading with their daughter from the bathroom.

Washing his hands, he walked into the room where he saw his wife pacing the floor with the baby, who's cries seem to be getting louder.

"Why is she crying like that?"

"I don't know. She's fed, burped and changed," his wife sighed. "I just need her to stop crying because she's driving me crazy."

"Give her to me. Maybe I can get her stop crying," Corey held his hands out.

"Nah. That's alright. I got her."

"Give me my daughter, Lyssa," Corey removed Alana from her hands.

"Corey, I'm telling you now. She's not gonna stop crying for---"

As soon as their daughter was comfortable in his arms, Alana's cries silenced immediately. Corey gazed down at his little girl as she started falling asleep in his arms. Corey glanced at Alyssa who was upset that he was able to get Alana to calm down. Without saying a word, she grabbed her phone and left out the room. Shaking his head, Corey waited until his baby girl was fully asleep before kissing her forehead and placing her in the crib. As he watched his daughter sleep, Corey chuckled at his wife's pettiness. Just because their daughter missed her dad, Alyssa got in her feelings. He didn't know if she was using this against him, but he had a feeling that he'd be paying for this in one way or another.

Sitting down in a nearby chair, Corey laced up his Nike boots then tucked his cell phone in his pocket. Since discovering that Julian was crooked and the fact that he lied about how he knew Larry, he felt the need to pop up at the rehab to see if he would catch the two of them together again. Even though Julian went into hiding, Corey thought that he might still be visiting Larry. Zipping up his hoodie, he grabbed his keys on his way out the room. He let his brothers know that he was making a quick run before leaving the house and hopping into his car. The car ride to the rehab was longer than usual due to a traffic and an accident on I-285. Arriving an hour later, Corey parked and killed the engine. He saw Deana in the parking lot talking on her phone and waited until she was out of sight to get out. Strolling to the entrance, he signed in and waited for the nurse to give him the okay to go back.

"Mr. Washington, I'm sorry to inform you that Larry is no longer with us at this facility," the flirtatious nurse from the last visit informed him.

"He left?"

"Actually, he was signed out a few days ago."

"Signed out? By who?"

"His nephew."

"His nephew? A nigga named Julian?" he blurted out.

"That information is confidential."

"Aight. Thanks," Corey left, making his way back to his car.

Bringing his car to life and removing his phone from his pocket, Corey shot a text to his brothers, letting them know that Larry was on the loose and was signed out by his so called nephew before pulling out of the lot with screeching tires into traffic. He was angry when he learned that the nigga his brothers brought in to help out with shit was dirty but finding out that Larry was signed out by his *"nephew"* had his mind racing a mile a minute. It seemed like as soon as they defeated one enemy, they gained another one. For a brief moment, Corey felt like Larry could've been looking out for him, but now, Larry had been added to the list of enemies they already had. As he drove down the expressway, Corey decided to stop at the mall to shop for his wife. With all the drama that had taken place since he'd been in rehab, he almost forgot that his one year anniversary was coming up in a couple of weeks. He cracked a smile at the thought of being married for a year. To him, it seemed like yesterday he'd just proposed to Alyssa. He remembered taking her out to eat at nice restaurant in New York and the look on her face when he asked her to be his wife. Corey wasn't sure what her answer was going to be, but he was damn glad when she said yes. Since the day they got engaged, shit between them had been rocky as hell—from finding out that she was an FBI agent to him possibly getting someone pregnant to her being overly flirty with her boss. Looking back over all the obstacles they overcame, it was easy for him to laugh about their problems now.

When he arrived at the Lennox Mall, he hit up BCBG, Louis Vuitton, Fendi and the jewelry store and ordered a customized diamond tennis bracelet, matching necklace, earrings, and anklet. After spending nearly two hours shopping for himself, his wife, and daughter, Corey caught the eye of every damn woman that was entering the mall on his way out. Piling the bags in the trunk, Corey hopped behind the wheel and headed home. Leaving Alyssa bags in the car, he went inside the house with two handful of bags, heading straight upstairs to their room where he found Alyssa singing to Alana on the bed. Corey noticed his wife glancing at the bags in his hands and smirked.

"How are my two favorite girls doing?" he placed the bags on the floor before sitting next to his wife and kissing her forehead.

"We're good," she replied. "I just gave her a bath and fed her."

"Cool," he said as he was about to pick Alana.

"Not uh. Go wash your hands first," Alyssa pointed to the bathroom.

Doing as he was told, Corey turned the water on and peeked into the room and saw Alyssa looking through the shopping bags and chuckled. When he was finished washing his hands, he felt the death stare that Alyssa was giving him but he ignored it. Picking his daughter up, she instantly smiled at him.

"So, you really went to the mall and only went shopping for you and Alana?" she pouted.

"I thought about getting you something but figured you wouldn't accept it being as though you're mad at me."

"You are so inconsiderate. I can't stand you," she huffed.

"Call it what you want but if the shoe was on the other foot, you wouldn't have brought me shit either," he glared at her.

Defeated, Alyssa folded her arms across her chest. After fifteen minutes of silence, she stormed out the room and Corey couldn't help but to laugh out loud. His baby girl continued to stare up him.

"Don't worry about your mom, lil mama. She's mad at me now, but she'll love me again soon enough. I just hope she doesn't kill me before our anniversary."

31

It took a lot of convincing, but while everyone had their own shit going on, Mari pretty much *demanded* that his wife go out with him. Ever since shit went left the month before, they hadn't had a date night and it was one of the things that she valued, so he decided to try his best to get back to the basics. Mari made reservations at Ruth Chris for eight o'clock and they were both dressed and out of the door by a quarter to seven. Even though he had some shit that he wanted to address with Drea himself, he held his composure and decided to at least wait until they made it to the restaurant and were in a neutral setting. That alone, he hoped would keep him level headed.

Mari had some slow jams playing as they made their way to the restaurant. Drea sat in the passenger's seat mostly on her phone and he was willing to bet the Holiday Sisters chat was full of pettiness. He chuckled at the thought but kept driving. A few minutes later, Drea's phone rang and she declined the call. It rang again and she picked up, giving her best friend Hannah a cheerful greeting. Mari knew good and damn well that it wasn't Hannah's call that she declined a few moments prior and the thoughts that he had caused him to clench his jaws. Drea talked to her BFF the rest of the ride to the restaurant, and D'Mari got lost once again in his thoughts.

At five minutes before eight, the couple was being seated in a booth and for the first time that night, Drea smiled. Mari ordered a bottle of wine for her and wasted no time ordering some brown liquor on the rocks for himself. Both of them stared at the menu in silence. If you didn't know any better, you would think that they were on their first date or some shit.

"Thanks for joining me," Mari finally broke the silence.

"Thanks for inviting me and being persistent."

The waitress returned with their drinks along with water and then took their orders for appetizers and entrees. As soon as she left, Mari took a big gulp of his drink and relaxed before he began addressing his concerns.

"Do you love me Andrea?"

"Huh... why would you ask me that?" she queried after taking a sip of wine.

"Why you pause? It's a simple question though... so you love me?"

"Of course I love you," Drea replied.

"Are you still *in love* with me?" Mari continued.

"Yes D'Mari... even though I've been pissed off at some things that have happened, my love for you hasn't changed. You have to look at this shit from my point of view as well. We have a family and you out in the streets, and I have to worry about whether you're gonna make it home to us every night. It's a lot to deal with. This is all new to me," Drea said and wiped the tear that was threatening to fall from her right eye.

"My life is complicated babe, I can't even lie and say it ain't. It's been that way since way before I met you. I fucked up and allowed what I do to harm you, and I'll live with that regret for the rest of my life. I'm thankful that you're still here wit us and I'll die trying to protect you from any bullshit Drea. I just don't need you to lose faith in me. *Don't stop loving me*," Mari expressed.

Mari reached across the table and grabbed Drea's hand and squeezed it. He stared into those beautiful eyes that he had fallen in love with. Mari was battling with asking her about his suspicions or just letting the shit go. It seemed as if the ice had been broken and they were headed in the right direction and he didn't want to go backwards; but it was gonna be hard as hell to let it go. He decided to change the subject momentarily and then decide on what to do later. The waitress brought their appetizers and sat them down in front of them. They wasted no time digging in and Mari shifted the conversation.

"I need your help with something."

"Anything for you," Drea replied and seductively licked her fingers.

Mari's dick bricked up and he was ready to skip dinner and go straight for dessert.

"Imma hold you to that shit when we get to the room."

"Room?" she quizzed.

"Yeah I booked us a room just to get away for the night. We ain't slept in on a Saturday in forever and we both need it."

"Sounds good Mr. Mitchell, but what do you need help with?

"J.R.'s situation... I don't necessarily want you on the case because it'll be a conflict of interest, but I need you to find the best lawyer to help us out," Mari explained.

"I definitely know the best... does it matter who it is?" Drea asked.

"If they the best... I trust you."

"Okay... I'll make the call tomorrow," Drea replied.

They stuffed their faces and talked and laughed like old times. Mari couldn't wait to get his wife to the room and make love to her, then fuck her, and then make love to her again. He could feel himself bricking up again at the thoughts of her pelvic muscles squeezing his dick.

"I'm ready to get outta here babe, but I gotta ask you one more question... actually two but one for now. Did you know that you were pregnant?"

"Of course not... I had been drinking and shit remember. My OB said the birth control threw my cycle off. I was sad about it, but Hannah said God knows best. My old ass don't need no more kids," Drea tried to laugh it off, but Mari could tell that she was still hurt.

"Come on baby... let's get out of here," he left three hundred dollars on the table and they headed towards the door.

"Well well well... we all finally meet at the same time," a voice said as soon as they walked outside.

D'Mari turned to his right and saw Janice standing with a man that he assumed was her husband. He had put that situation on the back burner only for it to pop up any damn way. He looked at Drea and noticed the worried look on her face.

"Don't look so shocked right now Mrs. Andrea... *you* been talking to *my husband* more than *me* so speak now," Janice taunted.

"You fuckin' this nigga Drea?" Mari fumed.

"Hell no D'Mari... are you serious right now?"

"This the second time this bitch done said..."

"Oh I'm a bitch when I was just tryna help you? I got receipts and I'll get the rest of 'em to you soon D'Mari," Janice stated.

"Janice... you need some fuckin' help. Let's go," the man finally broke his silence.

Mari stared him down and was pissed that he didn't have his heat on him. He headed to the car without waiting on Drea. She called out to him, but Mari was too pissed to wait on her.

"I wish I could explain," Drea said as soon as she got in.

"Don't wish... do the shit. This bitch done accused you of *fuckin'* her husband on multiple occasions and *you can't say shit*? All that mouth you got, but you can't defend yourself?"

"I can't D'Mari... it's complicated, but I swear to you I'm not fuckin' him," Drea pleaded.

"So you think Imma sit back and be aight wit that bullshit answer? You got me all the way fucked up," Mari retorted.

"You said *multiple* occasions? How many times you been wit that psycho bitch anyway?"

"Fuck all that... don't try to flip this shit on me!" Mari banged his hand on the steering wheel.

"You know what... we do more fighting than anything. It seemed like things were getting better and now look. Maybe we just aren't *meant to be*. I'm sick of all this arguing and shit. I didn't sign up for this bullshit," Drea cried.

"Maybe you right," Mari replied and turned the music up to the max, letting Drea know that the conversation was over.

He didn't want to lose his family, but maybe co-parenting was the best option because he couldn't be with anyone he didn't trust. Instead of going to the room that he had booked, Mari drove back to the house. When he pulled up, Drea got out and he left with no particular destination in mind. He just needed to get away.

32

D'Mani stood in the kitchen reheating the salmon that he'd gotten for Cheyanne earlier that day. It was a little after dinner, and everybody was off in the house doing their own thing. He was starting to think that maybe she might beat this thing. The most that ever happened since she got there was her feeling weak, maybe losing her breath here and there, and minor pain in her chest. She didn't look as bad as she did that day in the hospital either, and he was thankful that she wasn't always so tired anymore because Imani wanted to spend more time with her other than in her bedroom. He hadn't gotten around to talking to Cheyanne about them having a serious discussion with Imani about her condition, and he hoped that they wouldn't have to if she continued to do better. That wasn't something that he was ready to do even though he'd thought that he was. There was no easy way to tell a toddler that her mother was dying. D'Mani already knew that it would crush her to have just gotten her dad in her life, only to lose her mom.

D'Mani was snapped out of his thoughts by the sound of

the microwave beeping, and he went to put the soup on a tray for her. He also grabbed a bowl of cut up oranges, red apples, and cherries with a tall glass of tomato juice, which he knew she hated. It was best for her to have healthy choices and everything that he was serving would give her more energy, and had been said to be good for the heart.

He carried the tray up the stairs to where Cheyanne was resting with Imani and was stopped in his tracks at the sight of Anastasia standing outside of her bedroom. His first mind was to snap out about her creeping around the house and spying on people, but her body language stopped him. He could faintly hear Cheyanne talking, and he knew by the tone of her voice that she was trying to hold back tears as Imani asked her where she was going. It broke his heart to hear her tell their baby that she would be going to heaven and that Imani would stay here with him and Anastasia.

"Anastasia's going to take very good care of you baby girl. She'll do your hair, and play Barbie with you, and when you get older, she'll talk to you about boys and help you get ready for your first date, and then prom, and one day, when you're all grown up, she'll help daddy give you away at your wedding."

"But I don't like boys mommy... ugh, only Kyler. Will he be there?" Imani's little chipmunk pitched voice asked innocently. Cheyanne laughed. He could imagine that they were laid back on the bed with her stroking Imani's hair softly.

"You will one day. Your daddy won't like it much, but one day... you will, and Kyler will be there. They're going to all be there for you, and they'll remind you of how much I loved you, so you won't ever forget."

"Mommy, I ain't gone forget you! You're my mommy!"

"You're not going to forget me Mani.... I pray that's true baby." It was really quiet after that aside from the heavy breathing of Imani, letting him know that she was falling asleep. D'Mani's heart ached for both his baby mama and his daughter. That had to have been a hard conversation for Cheyanne to have with her, and she'd done it alone. Knowing Imani and how easily she had accepted what she'd told her, baby girl probably didn't believe her, or worse, she didn't understand that death meant her mother would no longer be there. He went to get Anastasia's attention, upset now that she had eavesdropped on such an emotional and serious moment between them, but she lightly tapped on the door and stepped inside. D'Mani eased closer and sat outside the door, setting the tray down beside him on the floor.

"I...don't know what to say Cheyanne." She spoke quietly and he could hear the regret in her voice. "I'm so sorry for being such a bitch this whole time. I guess I was being selfish over D'Mani."

"It's okay, I understand."

"No, it's not! I was wrong, and I was a mean, petty bitch... girl be honest."

"Yeah you were kind of." Cheyanne finally admitted and they both let out a chuckle.

"Oh I definitely was, ain't no kind of."

"Well, I guess I could understand your point of view. I owe you a big apology also."

"Let's not even bring that up again, and we can call a truce. I realize that we don't have to be best friends, but we don't gotta be enemies either." Anastasia said, causing D'Mani to smile. He was proud of her, even though it took her sneaky ass spying on Cheyanne.

"Truce." Cheyanne agreed. He wanted to assume that the silence that followed meant that the two were hugging it out, but he knew they hadn't gotten there quite yet.

"Well, I'll let you get your rest..."

"Okay.."

As Anastasia stepped out of the room, D'Mani stood

there. She jumped in surprise at the sight of him, and he motioned for her to wait a minute. Grabbing the tray, he took it into the room, ignoring the knowing look that Cheyanne was giving him.

"Yo nosy ass." She finally quipped after she realized that he wasn't going to say anything.

"I wasn't being nosy, I was bringing you this food that's probably cold as shit now, but the fruits still good. How you feelin'?" he asked, pleased that despite her sounding tired, she seemed to have a glow going on.

"I'm good, I actually feel good today. I know I won't be after I eat that nasty shit."

"Girl, this good for you." He argued with a laugh. "Just eat it and I'll be back in a little bit to check on you." She nodded silently and started eating out of the fruit bowl as he left out of the room. He made sure to close the door tight as he met Anastasia out in the hall. As soon as he stopped in front of her, she pulled him into a tight hug.

"I'm sorry I've been being so extra. I heard her talking to Imani about having to stay with us and, it was like... as a mother, I put myself in her shoes. If I had to leave Kyler, I would be beside myself. And even though I been being so fuckin' mean, she still didn't talk about me like I wasn't shit. How could I keep holding this grudge like this and the girl literally is leaving her daughter in our hands?!" she rambled damn near hysterically.

"Calm down, Ma. I can't say the way you been acting is okay, cause it ain't, but I'm glad that you finally see what I been telling you this whole time." He held her and ran his hands up and down her back, trying to soothe her. It was clear that what she had overheard had her shook up, and D'Mani couldn't say that he felt bad about her finally seeing Cheyanne's point of view. In his opinion, he wished that it had happened a little bit sooner, and maybe she wouldn't have wasted so much of their time on this petty bullshit; but he was willing to take let all of that old shit go if she was. Although D'Mani was hopeful that Cheyanne would pull through, he still didn't want to add any more stress in her life. And with Anastasia finally getting some act right, things may have been looking up for them all.

33

If you would have asked him five years ago if he'd settle down, J.R. would have looked at you like you was crazy. Going down to the court last minute and unprepared was one of the best things they could have done. J.R. promised her a big wedding once all the street shit was handled but Lexi declined. Further letting him know he had made the right choice.

Amir was getting bigger by the day. J.R. was grateful that he was able to be around and witness his growth first hand. Being parents of a newborn didn't really affect J.R. and Lexi how it would other couples their age. They had so much support that it took so much weight off of their shoulders.

Since getting married, J.R. had been around much more. He realized how his absence affected the ones he loved. D'Mari also schooled him on the time Drea dealt with postpartum depression and he would never want Lexi to experience that. Getting himself on track mentally, J.R. was now able to face the streets with a clear mind.

Pulling in front of the house in Bankhead, J.R. killed the engine, checked his surroundings and gun before exiting the vehicle. He did a quick jog up the porch and into the house where everyone greeted him. After checking on a few things with his boys, he made his way to the room where Jessica was kept. Knocking on the door twice, Jessica finally instructed for him to come in.

J.R. entered the quiet dark room and wondered why she was laying around like that. Walking over to the large window, J.R. pulled the curtains back slightly, allowing sunbeams to enter.

"Why you laying around in the dark?" he asked, now focusing on Jessica who laid in the bed with the covers over her head.

After a few moments of silence, J.R. walked over to her and pulled the covers back. Jessica scrambled to hide her face, but it was too late. J.R. had already seen the tears. Throughout the months, the two of them had grown close and Jessica never showed a sign of weakness until that very moment. Unsure of what to say, J.R. just spoke.

"You good? What's wrong?" he quizzed.

"Nothing, I'm fine." She lied.

J.R. walked over to the corner of the room, grabbed a chair, and scooted it across the floor. Stopping directly in front of her, he flopped down and began to pry.

"Look, I know I got you caged off in here, but I have my reasons. However, that don't mean you can't talk to me."

J.R. waited for a response but instead, Jessica just cried. He knew something had to really be bothering her and for some odd reason, he cared.

"Aight. When you want to talk, have one of the guys hit me up, and I'll slide back through." He stated, standing up from the chair but was stopped by Jessica's hand tugging at his arm.

"I miss my kids." She whispered softly, lowering her head.

To J.R., Jessica was this ride or die killer bitch. It had

slipped his mind this whole time that she had a life and family before he kidnapped her. A part of him started to feel bad, but he had to do what he had to do.

"I'm sorry Jes---"

"You don't have to be sorry, I did this to myself. I should have listened to your mom when she tried to help me out. I should have gotten out because of my kids but I didn't. I became this grimy bitch for Grant and what did Grant do for me? Not a damn thing but keep me his side bitch for years. HOW WAS I THE SIDE BITCH WHEN I WAS HERE FIRST?!" she screamed.

It was crazy how J.R.'s sole purpose for that visit was to get information about Grant out of Jessica and here she was, a woman scorned, ready to risk it all.

"It'll be alright. Once I kill these niggas, you'll be home with your kids." He assured her but Jessica only smacked her lips.

J.R. sat and analyzed everything. He was really beginning to feel bad. He wished it was more that he could do, but he had been crossed so many times that he trusted no one.

"Your kids........ are Grant in their lives?" he randomly asked, not sure himself where the question came from.

"Tuh! He's there finically but that's about it. Grant only cares about that dead bastard he got with his wife." She snapped.

"Dead bastard?" J.R. chuckled.

"Yup! They had a son but he died, died on my triples' birthday and every year, instead of being with us, he's at the cemetery." She explained.

"Damn...." was all J.R. mustered up to say.

"And that's why I'm so sick because my babies' birthday next week and neither mommy or daddy will be there." She began sobbing uncontrollably.

Over all the loud crying, J.R. couldn't help but peep how she said the triples' birthday was as close as next week.

"Aye Jessica. Do you know what cemetery his son buried at?" J.R. quizzed.

"Yes.... Oakland Cemetery right off of Oakland Ave...... why?"

A smile the size of *The Joker's* invaded J.R.'s face as he put his next plan in motion. He looked at Jessica who looked on confused and smiled at her as well.

"GET UP!" he yelled, jumping out of the chair and turning on the lights, but Jessica didn't move.

"GET THE FUCK UP!" he screamed, this time causing her to jump.

"You'll be there for their birthday. Get dressed! I'll call you an Uber so you can go home." He explained while Jessica stood frozen with her mouth to the floor.

"Oh my God J.R., thank you!" she yelled, moving swiftly about the room.

"But what about Justin? Even after you get Grant, won't you need me to get him too? That was the plan." She stopped and asked.

"You've helped me more than I could have imagined. I got the shit in the bag from here. Go be with your kids."

Jessica ran over and hugged J.R. as tight as her fragile body could. He wrapped one arm around and made her finish getting her shit together. Standing off to the corner, J.R. pulled out his phone and answered an incoming call from Corey.

"Wad up?" he sounded into the phone.

"It's like this nigga Larry dropped off the face of the Earth." Corey said from the other end.

"I ain't trying to hear that shit. How can a nigga go from being in rehab to vanishing without a trace? There has to be some type of information on him. What's the nigga full name? I'll put my people on it." J.R. replied.

"Larry Brumfield is the name he used in there."

"Larry Brumfield.... Larry Brumfield..... Aight text that to me and I'll check on it when I leave here." J.R. said, ending the call.

He placed the phone in his pocket and looked over at Jessica, who stood in the middle of the floor staring at him.

"WHAT?" he asked loudly.

"Di--- did--- you --- just----say----Larry---- Larry----Brumfield?" She stuttered, her face filled with fear.

34

Valentine's day had arrived, and it was hard for Corey to keep his plans for Alyssa a secret. She went back to not speaking to him when he made her believe that he didn't buy her nothing at the mall; but when he sent her out for a day of pampering the day before, his wife eased up a little bit. Enough for her to allow Corey to eat her pussy and that's all. Instead of being in his feelings, he let it ride because he knew that Alyssa was going to be singing a different tune when she found out what he had planned for their anniversary.

Corey got up early that morning and cooked breakfast for the women in the house. Strawberry waffles, sausages, ham, and cheese omelets with cheese grits was what he prepared, and when he was finished, Corey carried a tray of food up to their room. Two bouquets of red roses in vases sat on each of the nightstands and the gifts that he'd been hiding in the back of his truck rested at the foot of the bed. Placing the tray beside Alyssa on the bed, Corey began kissing and licking her neck to wake her up. Soft moans left her lips.

"Stop Corey. I'm trying to sleep," she said, not putting up much of a fight.

"Well stop trying. I need you to get up and eat, ma."

"Huh?" she opened her eyes to look at him.

"Happy Anniversary bae," he smirked.

Alyssa's mouth dropped at the sight of the roses, shopping bags, and breakfast.

"Aww bae, you made me breakfast in bed," she cooed. "I can't even remember the last time you cooked for me," Alyssa smiled.

"I know it's been awhile."

"And you went shopping?" When did you have time to do all this?"

"These bags have been sitting in my trunk since I went to the mall that day," he laughed.

"You are so wrong for that," Alyssa hit his arm.

"Well go head and eat. We got a plane to catch at one and you still gotta pack and whatever you don't have, we can buy when we get to Miami," he pecked her lips then got up from the bed.

"Miami? What about the baby?"

"There is more than enough women in this house who can look after lil mama. She'll be fine, Lyssa."

Nodding her head, Alyssa grabbed the tray and ate her food while Corey dipped into the bathroom to take a shower. When Corey was finished with his hygiene, he walked into the bedroom, grabbed his suitcase, and began to pack. Feeling his wife's eyes him, Corey wanted to take advantage of the moment but decided to wait until they were alone. When he was finished packing, he got dressed in a black Polo tee shirt, light denim Balmain jeans, and black Louis Vuitton sneakers.

Placing his suitcase by the door, Corey walked over to the crib where Alana was laying there wide awake. He picked her up, cradled her in his arms, and sat in the nearest chair. The love he had for his little girl was beyond words. Although she was only six weeks old, Corey felt like Alana knew when he was there and when he wasn't. He hated being away from his baby girl but when he came home from being in the streets all the, holding her in his arms melted away all of his frustration.

Corey handled all of the baby's needs while his wife prepared for their trip. By noon, they were all packed and ready to go. As they made their way out the door, Alyssa was finding it hard to say good-bye to Alana. After ten minutes of good-bye, Corey placed their luggage in the trunk of the limo before sliding inside next to his wife.

"Corey, I don't know about this. I don't feel comfortable leaving Alana," Alyssa sighed.

"Baby, believe me when I tell you, she'll be fine," he kissed her cheek. "Aight?"

"Okay," she nodded her head before resting it on his shoulder. "To be honest bae, I thought you forgot about our anniversary."

"Are you serious?" he glanced down at her.

"I mean you spend so much time in the streets doing God knows what and not to mention your lil girlfriend from the rehab... I didn't think you would remember," Alyssa sarcastically spat.

"Alyssa, let me set ya ass straight on something right now, Shawty from the rehab meant *nothing* to me. Did she have a thing for me? Yeah. Was I wrong for asking her to run errands for me? Maybe but at the end of day, nothing happened between us that's worth you being upset about. I love ya ass Alyssa and I wouldn't do anything to fuck up my marriage and lose my family. So if you wanna hold a grudge and have an attitude over nothing, *fine* but don't bother me with that shit. Matter of fact, get off me," Corey slid to the other side of the limo.

Ignoring the stunned look on Alyssa's face, he inserted his wireless ear buds into his ears and listened to music the rest of the ride to the airport. When they arrived forty minutes later, the driver popped the trunk and opened the door for them. Corey tipped the driver before grabbing the suitcases from the trunk, leaving Alyssa's on the sidewalk for her to get as he made his way inside. He walked ahead of her until they reached their gate and when she caught up to him, Alyssa tried to talk to him but he ignored her. Corey was tired of her shit and didn't want to be bothered with his wife at the moment. He just needed some time to himself.

Boarding the plane, they took their seat in first class. Alyssa glanced out of the window while Corey slept the entire flight. Nearly two hours later, their flight landed in Miami. They grabbed their luggage from baggage claim then made their way towards the exit where another limo was waiting for them. The Miami weather was very warm and humid. A big difference from Georgia, where is it was currently cold. Climbing inside the limo, the driver drove twenty minutes to the Miami Marriott Biscayne Bay. Grabbing their bags out the trunk, Corey checked them in, got their key cards, and went up to their room.

As soon as he closed the door, he was caught off guard by Alyssa's actions. She threw her arms around his neck, kissing him passionately. Dropping everything in his hands, Corey wrapped his arms around her, welcoming her tongue into his mouth. Unbuttoning his jeans, Alyssa slid his boxers and jeans down to his ankles, stroking his big, thick shaft.

"What's all this?" he questioned, breaking their kiss.

"Just shut up and enjoy it," Alyssa smiled seductively.

Dropping to her knees, she pushed all nine inches of his dick to the back of her throat, sliding him in and out of her mouth.

"Fuucckk!" Corey groaned as he watched his wife do her thing.

Alyssa massaged his balls with her hand as she continued to deep throat his manhood. The moans along with the slurping sounds she made drove him crazy. Corey grabbed a handful of her hair and began fucking her mouth and she took everything like a pro. Feeling himself about to bust, Corey pulled his wife up to her feet, bent her over, lifted her dress, moved her thong to the side, and slammed his dick inside her, causing her to gasp. Gripping her hips, he pounded away at her tight wet pussy. He fucked her roughly with long deep strokes which had Alyssa making noises Corey never heard her make before.

"Yeesss Daddy! Fuck this pussy!"

Slapping her ass, he went deeper and harder inside her. It wasn't long before her legs began to shake and seconds later, Alyssa came all over his dick. Corey knew that she couldn't take anymore but he wasn't stopping. He continued his punishment until she came for the same time and he filled her insides with cum minutes later. Too exhausted to move, they stood posted up against the front door for a few moments before Corey walked them to the bathroom where they cleaned up. Corey smiled at the way his wife staggered out the bathroom when she was finished cleaning herself up, but little did she know, he was far from done with her ass. Alyssa kept the pussy away from him for weeks, and Corey needed to make up for lost time and punish his wife for her fucked up behavior.

35

The Rock Boyz hadn't handled the shit that they needed to handle in the streets, but Mari knew that they all needed a break from everything. Corey's ass was the only one who had dipped off, but it was for his anniversary, so it was understandable. The couples had made up, well most of them. Him and Drea weren't back on track, but he hoped that they would be soon. He decided to just give the shit time and stop trying to force it. Just for the night, the guys decided to hang out with each other and not discuss relationship problems or work, but they were still working. The four of them were gathered in Lexi's office at HS4 helping J.R. with the orders and shit. The manager that Lexi hired had been doing a hell of a job, but it was nothing like being around your own shit, so Mari suggested they make an appearance and then kick back without their mates for a few hours. The girls must have wanted some time without them as well because none of them put up a fuss and that was rare.

"This club is cleaning up the money pretty damn good," Mari announced.

"I knew yo ass was finna get into business sooner or later," Mani chuckled.

"Shut the hell up... I was just sayin'," Mari replied as he finished going over the books.

"Y'all know that nigga gon' be working... when he ain't at work?" Corey chimed in.

"Well had you stayed on top of yo shit, this would be you doin' this shit and not me," Mari fired back and caused all of the guys to erupt into laughter.

"Fuck all y'all... I done got my shit together. When y'all gon' let that shit die?" Corey retorted.

The other three guys all paused and looked as if they were in deep thought.

"NEVER!" they said unison and the laughter continued.

"Muthafuckas...I already gotta hear Aunt Shirley's mouth all the damn time. Do y'all know she actually be grabbing her purse like I'm a fuckin' crackhead for real?" Corey expressed and all of the guys couldn't control their laughter.

"That old lady something serious, but she real as fuck," J.R. added and they all agreed.

"Aight y'all... let's get out here and see what's poppin'," Mani told them.

"Shots up for the muthafuckin' Rock Boyz!" Mari poured everyone another round and they all downed them instantly.

The guys made their way from the office and dispersed to the main floor. It was a Friday night and it was packed as hell. The music had everyone vibing and of course the strippers were doing their thang, draining the pockets of the men with ease. Out of nowhere, Mari spotted some commotion in the right corner. By instinct, his hand went right to his gun. Before he could do anything else, security had the situation under control and they were escorting a dude out. All of the guys were in desperate need of a chill night out without any problems, but it didn't seem like that shit was going to happen.

Another hour passed with no problems. The guys were gathered around the bar when an *eerie* feeling came upon Mari. He felt someone staring at him and turned to his left and his blood began to boil. Normally he could figure out the angles of bitches, but he was thrown for a loop with that one and was sick and tired of the games.

"Imma just have to kill this bitch once and for all," he mumbled to himself and began to mentally prepare on how he was going to execute the shit.

36

Since the women had their heart to heart, D'Mani had to say that he'd seen a big shift in the overall mood between them. It wasn't all peaches and cream, but it was definitely better than it had been. Really, it seemed like things were looking up for everybody in the house and he couldn't lie and say that it wasn't nice to not have so much friction, but there was still the matter of their enemies lingering. Since they were getting closer to eliminating the problem, D'Mani felt confident taking his family out to eat and for a night of fun. He, Anastasia, Cheyanne, Imani, and Kyler all loaded into the car and headed out to the Georgia Aquarium. The kids were super excited since they hadn't really been going out much besides school and daycare, and he was just as excited as they were.

When they arrived at the Aquarium, he noted that it was really busy and hoped that it wouldn't be a problem for Cheyanne to be surrounded by so many people and wild ass kids. Without even saying anything, he decided that if she even looked a little tired, he would take her home. D'Mani popped the trunk and pulled out the wheelchair that he'd put there as everyone filed out of the car and instantly, Cheyanne gave him the stank face.

"I'm not sittin' in that!" she said, immediately shaking her head in defiance.

"Cheyanne, it's big as fuck in there. I just don't want you to get tired trying to keep up with the kids."

"I'll be okay, but I ain't sittin' in that damn wheelchair." They stood there staring each other down, neither one ready to let go of their stance until finally Anastasia stepped in between them.

"Why don't you just leave it out here and if she does get tired, then you can come get it D'Mani." She suggested simply.

"That's cool, but I know I'm not going to be tired. I've been feeling really energized lately, this lil trip ain't gone be nothin'."

D'Mani didn't believe that for a second, but he didn't want to upset her. It seemed like it was a big deal for her not to feel as if she wasn't capable of doing things, and he could understand that considering how strong of a woman she was. But at the same time, he didn't want that strength to have her out there passing out, considering that she had pretty much been on bed rest since she'd moved into the house. Her and Anastasia looked at him, waiting to see if he was going to put up any more of a fight, so he went ahead and put the wheelchair back. He noticed them share a conspiratorial smirk when they thought he wasn't looking, and he briefly wondered if it was going to be like this all the time, with them trying to double team him and shit.

They waited as he finished and locked up the car before they all went to stand in line, with him holding on to Kyler and Imani's hands while the two women walked a little ways ahead. D'Mani liked that they were getting along for the most part. They needed to talk and get to know each other in his opinion, and it would make things easier for everyone involved.

After he paid, both Kyler and Imani dragged him off to see the different displays of exotic fish. Along the way, they picked up all types of hats, sunglasses, and swords to play with. If he didn't know any better, he would have thought that they had previously discussed how they would drain his wallet. Occasionally, he would look back to see how Cheyanne and Anastasia were doing, and he was surprised to see that Cheyanne was still keeping up and not looking winded or tired at all. Maybe she was right about having more energy.

"Daddy! Daddy! I'm thirsty!" Imani said loudly, pulling at his hand.

"Yeah me too, do they got food?" Kyler asked.

"Yeah, they got food lil man. Let me see if y'all mamas want something." He told the kids before leading them back towards where Cheyanne and Anastasia stood looking at someone on the virtual voyager.

"Hey y'all having fun?" Cheyanne asked as soon as she noticed them.

"Yes! We saw some jellyfish, and clown fish, and Dori!" Imani bragged.

"That wasn't no Dori!" Kyler argued with his face scrunched up.

"Yeah it was!"

"Imani, it wasn't Dori. It was just the same kind of fish as her." D'Mani explained, still garnering a disappointed look from her.

"So, that wasn't Nemo either?"

"Naw it wasn't Nemo either." They all chuckled at her innocence.

"Told you." Kyler couldn't help but add.

"Look let's just go eat, cause y'all gone be at it all day." D'Mani said. "Was y'all ready to grab a bite too?"

"Hell yeah, you know I'm hungry, considering all those healthy alternatives you been giving me." Cheyanne joked.

"Same here." Stasia chimed.

"Well come on cause we were about to hit up the café." D'Mani ignored the comment about the food because in his opinion, it was the main reason she was walking around without losing her damn breath, but he would let it ride.

As they made their way over to where the café was located, he happened to look back in time to see Cheyanne stop in midstride with a pained look on her face. He immediately turned with the kids in tow and ran back in her direction as Anastasia screamed out his name and tried to help ease her to the floor.

By the time he made it to where they were, Cheyanne was on the ground holding her left arm and crying in pain. The crowd that surrounded them backed away and people were trying to get their children away from the scene.

"Mommy!" Imani cried.

"Stasia please take them to the car quick." D'Mani ordered as he pulled out his phone and dialed 911. Without argument, she dragged a kicking and screaming Imani away with Kyler running behind her. "Cheyanne it's gone be okay. I already called the ambulance ma." He tried to reassure her as she lay there breathing heavily. He took off the jacket that he was wearing and placed it under her head, trying to provide her with some type of comfort.

It seemed like it took the ambulance forever to get there; though he was sure it had only taken them maybe twenty minutes or so. As soon as he saw them making their way towards them, D'Mani stood up to give them some room.

"Yo what the fuck y'all doin'! Get her the fuck outta here!" he barked once he saw that they were trying to ask her questions and shit instead of putting her straight on a gurney. As if he was their boss, they did as he had asked after giving each other a look. D'Mani followed them out of the building and to the ambulance. He could see Stasia standing out there next to the car on her phone, crying.

"Stasia follow us... I'm riding with her to the hospital!" he shouted and then jumped into the back right behind the EMT's and Cheyanne. He wondered if this was the type of scene that Imani had saw when she'd had to call the ambulance for her mama. If so, he knew that she was terrified and he couldn't blame her because he was scared out of his mind. Give him a shoot out or an over dose and he rolled with the punches; but the sight of his baby mama on the floor clutching her arm with her eyes rolling to the back of her head, he was ready to faint. Though D'Mani wasn't really big on religion, he couldn't help, but to try talking to God as he watched them work on her. Even though they were supposed to be prepared for this scenario, he couldn't bring himself to accept death as her fate. Tears streamed down his face as he silently begged God to spare her for the sake of their child. There was just no way that she was about to die; he wouldn't be able to accept that. She had to pull through.

37

Corey was laid up in bed when he got a text from Mari telling him to meet him in the basement in an hour. Realizing that he was in the bed alone, he took that as an opportunity to get washed and dressed before Alyssa came in and began asking him a million and one questions about what he was getting into that day. Although things were going well between them, Alyssa was back to her worrying self since he was back in the streets. Whenever he had to handle business, Corey would check in just to let his wife that he was cool and when he would be home, but that didn't stop her from hugging him tightly when he came home and holding onto him for dear life when they were sleep. As much as Corey wanted Alyssa to ease up a little, he knew she wouldn't because she knew as well as he did that every time he walked out the door, he might not return home, but Corey, J.R., Mani and Mari were making sure they returned home to their families every night.

When he finished in the bathroom, he threw on a black Jordan sweat suit and matching Jordan's. Corey snatched up his keys and phone before walking out the room. As he made his way to the stair case, Alyssa met him at the top of the stairs with their daughter in her arms.

"And where you think you going?"

"I'm about to chill with my bros. We got some business to take care of today," Corey answered about to head down the stairs.

Alyssa sighed.

"Look ma, I know how you feel about me being back in the streets, but I'm handling business so we can be straight in the future."

"There are other ways you can make sure we're straight, Corey. By getting a real job again."

Corey sighed running his hand over his face.

"Baby, I don't mean to stress you out and I don't want to keep bringing up the past, but that's something you need to think about. You almost lost *everything* by being in the streets, and I don't wanna lose you again bae," Alyssa fought back tears.

"You're not gonna lose me bae," he gripped her chin, kissing her lips softly.

They embraced each other for few moments before releasing each other.

"Before you be gone for most of the day, can you get me a bag of hot Cheetos, a wild cherry Pepsi, and a couple of Slim Jim's from the store please?"

"Okay, Lyssa."

"Thank you baby," Alyssa kissed his cheek. "I'll see you when you get back."

Jogging down the stairs, he went to the basement where he found his brothers smoking a blunt.

"Aye. Wassup y'all?" Corey gave them handshakes before sitting down in the recliner chair.

"We're about to go run down on this nigga Grant. You rolling with us?" J.R. exhaled the weed smoke.

"Nigga what type of question is that? Of course I'm going."

"Aight. As soon as we finish this, we'll bounce," Mari added.

"By the time y'all finish that, I should be back from the store."

"The fuck you going to the store for?" J.R. asked.

"Alyssa wants snacks and shit," he sighed. "Let me go grab her stuff and I'll be right back."

"Hurry up man," Mari called out behind him.

Exiting the house, Corey jumped in his truck, bringing it to life. He pulled out of the driveway and drove down a few blocks down to the nearest gas station. The conversation he had with his wife briefly entered his mind but Corey quickly dismissed it. He couldn't let Alyssa's words distract him from what he was about to do that day. Arriving at the store, Corey parked on the side of the lot where the vacuum and air pump was. Before hopping out the car, an uneasy feeling suddenly came over him. Corey checked his surroundings to see if anything seemed out of the ordinary, but nothing stood out to him. Scanning his surrounding once more, he went inside the store, grabbing two of everything that his wife wanted.

After paying for Alyssa's snacks, Corey jogged back to his car and before he could get in his car, he was caught off guard by a blow to the back of his knees followed by a blow to his back. Dropping everything in his hands as he fell to the ground, he let out an agonizing scream. Corey tried to scramble to his feet but was kicked in stomach and stomped on his back. In between the stomps and kicks, Corey attempted to get up numerous times but to no avail. The pain from being kicked and stomped repeatedly caused him to get weaker by the minute. Stretched out on the ground, his attackers ended their attacks when a car came to a screeching halt beside him. Corey heard his phone ringing in his pocket as his attackers lifted him off the ground, tossing him in the open trunk. He tried to get a good look at his attackers but was unsuccessful when he was knocked unconscious.

38

D'Mani raced inside of the hospital behind the EMT's and prepared to run his ass right into the back with them too. They were still working on her as a crowd of doctors and nurses came and took over, each yelling out different medical terms to each other that he didn't understand.

"I'm sorry, but you can't go back there." One of the nurses said, jumping in front him and stopping him from following the stretcher through the double doors. D'Mani looked down at her hands on his chest and then back up at her face with a scowl that made her remove them from his body.

"Bitch I can go where ever the fuck I want to!" her eyes bucked in surprise, and she backed away which was good, because the way he felt, he might have thrown her ass somewhere.

"Baby, calm down." D'Mani hadn't even realized that Anastasia had already made it to the hospital. She gave him a soothing look and then nodded towards the kids who were standing nearby. "Don't scare them anymore than they already are." He visibly calmed down somewhat, letting Anastasia slip her arm through his.

"I'll let you know of any updates as soon as possible." The nurse chimed in, still keeping her distance from him. He nodded and then shrugged off to go and pick up Imani from where she was sitting in one of the stiff plastic chairs the hospital had in the waiting area. She looked like she was tired from the events of the day and from not having eaten anything. Kyler sat beside her with his hand in hers like a good big brother, looking just as tired and hungry as she did.

"I'm gonna go grab them something quick to eat from downstairs, you want anything?" D'Mani asked Stasia who was still clinging closely to his side. She shook her head slowly.

"Naw, I'm good, and I called Aunt Shirley to come and get the kids." She informed him, and if the situation wasn't so serious, he would have laughed. He didn't have anything against their Aunty, but her ass was too wild to be held responsible for some kids.

"Aunt Shirley though?" he asked with raised brows.

"Nigga don't do my Aunty! There's really nobody at the house right now, and she's the only one who can get away at the moment." She rolled her eyes and said.

D'Mani had forgotten that they were supposed to be riding down on niggas. With everything that was going on, it must have slipped his mind. He told Stasia to give him a second and went to call his brother to let them know what had happened. Of course D'Mari assured him that they could handle things without him, knowing that his place was there at the hospital, but he still didn't like the idea of not being there to have him and JR's backs. He didn't argue about it though and agreed that he would stay where he was to make sure Cheyanne was cool.

It didn't take Shirley long to arrive for the kids with a

couple of happy meals in her hands. Of course the kid's weary eyes lit up at the sight, and D'Mani made sure to let Imani know that he would be there to watch out for her mommy and how she was doing. It hurt him to know that he couldn't promise to bring her home, but he didn't want to lie to her. There was a chance that Cheyanne wouldn't make it and he didn't want his baby girl to feel like he had broken a promise. He gave her a kiss on her chubby little cheek and they were gone.

Maybe thirty minutes later, a doctor came out and asked for Cheyanne's family, and D'Mani jumped up, not wasting any time meeting him in the center of the room.

"Well, Cheyanne suffered a severe heart attack. We managed to stabilize her for now, but honestly with her condition, it will be touch and go for a while." The doctor said with a grim look on his face.

"Can I see her?"

"She's actually pretty sedated, but she was awake and asking to see a D'Mani?" he flipped through the chart and looked at D'Mani quizzically.

"That's me."

"Okay well, you can go ahead back, but I would advise that for now, we keep it at one person at a time." He put his clipboard under his arm and walked off.

"You go ahead bae." Stasia told him. "I'll wait right out here."

D'Mani silently nodded and made his way to the room that they said she was in. When he walked inside, his chest tightened at the sight of Cheyanne hooked up to all types of machines. She looked like she was sleeping with her hands down at her sides as she laid on her back.

"Come on in here." Her weak voice came out raspy, and he realized that she was watching him as he entered.

"How you feelin'? You know you just scared the shit out of

me right?" he joked, hoping to lighten the mood. He pulled a chair up right next to the bed and held her hand in his.

"Where's Imani, did I scare her really bad?" she asked as tears welled up in her eyes. He quickly wiped them away.

"It's okay, she went to the house with Aunt Shirley and she was a little worried, but baby girl knows you're a rider." He hoped to ease her worry, but from the look on her face, she was thinking the same thing he was when Stasia had told him about Shirley coming.

"Shirley?"

"That's the same thing I said." He chuckled. "She's good though, Drea should be at the house, and she came prepared with McDonald's." They both knew that a chicken nugget happy meal was the magic trick as far as their daughter was concerned. Cheyanne nodded and then she got really quiet before turning back to him.

"I know that I'm supposed to be prepared to die, knowing that its inevitable and all, but today when I felt that pain in my arm, I was scared. I thought that the last time my baby would see me would be today, and I hadn't told her that I loved her or how beautiful she looked."

"It's okay." He went to cut her off, but she held up a hand to stop him.

"No, it's not. I realize that I can't leave this place without getting some things off of my chest! There's something I need you to know!" she said, raising her voice. The action caused one of her machines to start beeping loudly and D'Mani glanced at it nervously, not sure of what was going on.

"It's cool, Cheyanne. You can tell me whatever it is later if it's causing you to get this worked up." He rubbed her hand and tried to get her to relax, but she shook her head as tears streamed down her face.

"I might not be able to tell you later! I need you to know

this... it's important!" D'Mani was torn between listening to whatever it was she was trying to say and forcing her to stop because it was obviously getting her too worked up. Figuring that maybe if she just got it out, she would calm down, so he decided to just let her tell him. He motioned for her to go ahead with a short nod.

"It's about Imani. She's not....." she started and then her body began shaking wildly and her eyes were rolling into the back of her head. D'Mani jumped out of his chair and ran over to the door.

"Aye I need some help in here... hurry up!" as a swarm of doctors ran in and shoved him out of the way. D'Mani felt helpless and despite what was going on, he wondered what about Imani had her so worked up that she had a seizure.

☙ 39 ❧

Jessica had slipped up and given the perfect opportunity for the guys to get at Grant. Mari was dressed in a pair of Balmain jeans and a gray hoodie. He felt bad for his twin having to deal with the situation with Cheyanne, but they still had to make a move. The opportunity might not present itself like that again. Even though Mani wanted to still go with them, the guys made him stay at the hospital with Cheyanne. The doctors had pretty much told them that there was nothing that could be done for her sickness, but Mari really hoped that she pulled through. Especially for Imani's sake. Anastasia had even taken the news hard because of the bond that her and Cheyanne developed within the past few weeks.

Mari called Corey for the fifth time and the nigga still didn't pick up the phone. He was only supposed to be running to the corner store to grab a few snacks for Alyssa, but he had been gone almost twenty minutes.

"That nigga ain't made it back yet?" J.R. entered the basement and queried.

"Nah... he must have had to go somewhere else or some

shit, but he should have let us know," Mari stated with agitation.

"Well look... shoot that nigga a text and tell him we out. We can handle that nigga anyway. He gon' be alone," J.R. stated.

Mari called Corey one more time, only to get the same results. He said *fuck it* and did what J.R. suggested and sent a text. Once that was done, the duo slipped out of the door and headed towards their destination. When their anthem came on, Mari and J.R. both rapped along with HOV and got into their zone. As he maneuvered through the streets, Mari noticed that they were a little behind schedule and he silently hoped that it wouldn't fuck up their plans. Even though they were planning to kill a nigga on a Sunday, they needed everything to go as planned.

"There that old ass nigga go right there!" Mari said as he drove slowly.

"Let's send him and that old ass trench coat to hell," J.R. chimed in.

Mari parked at an angle behind Grant and even though they knew they were strapped, they double checked and hopped out of the car. They slowly made their way towards Grant while his back was still to them.

"You wanna pop his ass now?" Mari quizzed.

"Nah... I want that nigga to look me in the eyes before I kill his ass. This shit is personal," J.R. replied.

"Say less. Let's go."

They got close as hell to Grant and then both of them got the shock of their lives at the words he spoke.

"What's up nephew?"

Both J.R. and D'Mari stopped dead in their tracks.

"If you was on the winning team, you wouldn't be going to meet yo maker today. I gotta give it to you, the way you got Elliot was commendable, but I ain't no weak bitch. I'm sure that bitch of mine told you I would be here, which is why in five... four... three... two...

Before Grant got to one, shots rang out and Mari and J.R. both began shooting too. Mari knew he hit Grant, but the nigga must have been wearing a vest because he never went down. A few seconds later, a burning sensation came over him and he felt himself becoming weak. Mari fought to keep his eyes opened and he tried not to panic. When he looked down and saw his sweatshirt drenched in blood, the burning got stronger and everything became blurry. Mari felt himself calling out for J.R., but little did he know, the words never left his mouth before darkness took over him.

40

Once the shots stopped and the tires screeched in the distance, J.R. slowly rose to his feet. He looked around, making sure the coast was completely clear before he proceeded.

"Aight we good my nigga. Let's bounce." He said, looking over at a motionless D'Mari.

The worst possible outcome invaded his thoughts, but he refused to even think that way.

"Aye Mari, I said get up!" J.R. voice grew louder as he walked slowly over to his brother.

When he made it closer, he noticed that D'Mari once gray hoodie was now crimson red. It was clear to a blind eye that he took a bullet to the chest and was losing a lot of blood.

"FUCKKKKK!" J.R. YELLED AT THE TOP OF HIS LUNGS before bending down and lifting Mari.

AS SCARED AS J.R. WAS TO MOVE HIM, HE KNEW THAT TIME was not on their side and he couldn't just sit there and wait. Using all the strength he had, he pulled Mari to the car. Once there, J.R. ran and opened both backdoors before lifting him inside and pulling him further in from the other side. After making sure he was secured, J.R. hopped in the car and sped off.

Too many times in the past months he had taken this same trip to the emergency room and just like the previous times, he blamed himself. Being *thirsty* got his brother shot. He knew better than to come at Grant Tessa without an army behind him. Had he just stopped and planned it out, that hit would have been easy, just like the first one.

J.R.'s thoughts plagued him the whole ride because before he knew it, he was at the hospital.

"BITCH YOU BET NOT DIE ON ME!" J.R. SAID aloud as he swung the door open.

AFTER YELLING FOR HELP, TWO HOSPITAL EMPLOYEES FLEW out the doors and aided him with transporting D'Mari. It was unclear how he was doing but he was breathing and that's all that mattered. J.R. gave all the information to the triage nurse while they rushed D'Mari to the back for surgery.

Pacing the waiting room floor back and forth, J.R. prepared to do the one thing he dreaded most.

"Hey baby. Is Drea around you?" he asked calmly, trying to disguise the hurt in his voice.

"Why J.R.? What's wrong?" Lexi buzzed from the other end.

"I need you to go give her the phone."

"Oh my God..... DREEEEAAAAAA!" Lexi yelled so loud in J.R's ear that he had to remove the phone.

"Baby, what's wrong? Are you ok? Where is Mari?" Lexi shot question after question until Drea must have snatched the phone from her hands.

"What's wrong?" she asked right away, catching J.R. off guard.

He paused for a moment and let out a deep breath before replying.

"Can y'all come to Emory Hospital right now?"

J.R. heard yelling and then the phone disconnected. He tried calling back but Lexi's phone went straight to voicemail. After those unsuccessful attempts, he called Corey's phone and got no answer, so he then dialed Mani's, who picked up on the first ring.

"Y'all good?" he asked as soon as they connected.

"Yo bro, where you at?" J.R. replied.

"Headed to the elevator, I'm still at the hospital with Cheyenne. What's up?"

"I'm at Emory too man, meet me in the lobby."

J.R. ended the call before Mani could ask any more questions and waited for the elevator doors to open. Once it did, Mani walked over to him in a panic.

"What's up? What's wrong? Where my brother?" he rambled on, looking around the empty waiting area.

"It's Mari bro. He was shot and I have no clue how he's doing. They rushed him into surgery about twenty minutes ago." J.R. explained.

"NOT MY TWIN MAN!" D'MANI SAID IN A LOW SOMBER tone which pierced J.R.'s heart because he too went through that with Yasmine, so he knew how he was feeling.

AS J.R. SEARCHED FOR THE RIGHT WORDS TO SAY, THE doors at the hospital slid open and in came Andrea, Anastasia, Alyssa, and Alexis. It was clear that the ladies had been crying, but Drea looked like she had been through hell and back, in just that short car ride.

"WHERE IS HE? WHERE IS MY HUSBAND?" SHE ASKED, HER eyes searching both J.R and D'Mani's.

JUST AS HE WAS ABOUT TO RESPOND, TWO DOCTORS BOTH IN white lab jackets appeared in front of them.

"UMMMM.... EXCUSE US BUT WE'RE LOOKING FOR THE family of Cheyenne Collins?"

D'MANI STEPPED FORWARD AND SO DID ANASTASIA, WHO latched onto his arm.

"WE'RE SORRY TO INFORM THE FAMILY THAT SHE HAS passed away. From everyone here at Emory, we send our condolences."

THE HOLIDAY SISTERS ALL BEGAN TO WEEP SOFTLY WHILE

D'Mani hugged Anastasia. J.R. stepped back and watched as his family hurt. Although Cheyenne passing had nothing to do with him, he still felt the guilt from all the tears and heartache he caused them. Feeling like the world was on his shoulders and no longer giving a fuck about nothing, J.R. stormed out of the hospital doors and to his car. He peeled off and headed right to the expressway. If it was war that the Tessa Cartel wanted, well *war* was what J.R. was going to give them. He planned on putting everything to rest that night.

Being that he was close to his old place, J.R stopped off there first. Since the crib was empty, J.R. kept all his guns locked away in a safe there. He knew that riding around with that type of fire power and being out on bond was not a good idea, but he was ready to risk it all.

Once he arrived, he hopped out, went inside, and went straight to work. J.R. packed up as much as he could inside two black duffle bags. He then went to his second safe and pulled out a couple bands of money, stuffed them in the bag as well, and headed down the stairs.

Once he made it to the middle of the stairway, the front doorbell rang. Upon scaring the fuck out of him, J.R. swiftly drew his gun and aimed it at the door. There was absolutely *no reason* why anyone should be ringing their bell when no one has been living in that house for months.

"Somebody followed me." He said to himself as the bell rang again.

"But who the fuck rings the doorbell?" He asked himself as he crept down the stairs.

Once he made it to the door, he stopped and contemplated his next move. If he opened it, someone could blow his brains out. If he didn't open it, someone could come in and blow his brains out. But either way, he rather look his killer in the eyes, so he swung the door open and came face to face with *death* itself.

TO BE CONTINUED...

Biittcchheess

March 30, 2019

Made in the USA
Middletown, DE
07 September 2021

47786649R00130